a love deferred

A KNIGHT TO LOVE

BOOK 2

BROOKELYN MOSLEY

more by brookelyn mosley

Links to the below stories can be found here (https://brookelynmosley.com/ebooks-paperbacks/)

Novels/Novellas/Novelettes/Series

- No Fraternizing, Pt. 1
- No Fraternizing, Pt. 2
- No Fraternizing, Pt. 3
- First Came Love: The Love, Hate & Revenge Prequel
- Love, Hate & Revenge, Pt. 1
- Love, Hate & Revenge, Pt. 2
- Love, Hate & Revenge, Pt. 3
- Girl Code
- Mr. & Mrs. Jones
- Forbidden: An Anthology
- They Call Me Mello
- A Love Deferred
- Indecent Arrangement
- Last Comes Love
- Ebb & Flow
- PRIDE
- Meant To Be
- LUST
- Loveless
- GREED
- Rekindled

- My First, My Last
- ENVY
- Ready or Not
- So This is Love
- Home Before Midnight
- GLUTTONY
- When Luke Met Juliette
- When Life Gives You Sunsets
- In Love, I Trust
- Wrath
- Sloth

Short Stories

- Unsilent Knight
- Twice In Love
- Home For Christmas

bybk exclusives

Bed Bully

Stuck

LHR Rewind Series

Home Before Midnight

Maybe This Time Will Be Different

Lovekilla

Incoming Call

Rough

WYD

Drinks on Me

Cali & Lee

Ray & Jay

Living Out a Love Song

Glimpses

One Mic

With Love, Ayanna & Dallas

Just Friends

Lena's Ex-File

Dream Boss

Chateau Luxure

Click Here to see if new exclusive shorts have been added to ByBK

(Copy + paste this link if the above link doesn't work: https://bybrookelynmosley.com/collections/ebooks)

acknowledgments

A loving thank you to my amazing husband who is without a doubt one of my biggest supporters. Your support is worth its weight in gold. A special thank you to my reading family. To the active members in my Brookelynites Cafe Facebook reading group, my beloved beta readers, and my supporters across all social medias. You all have embraced my brand of writing and I'm beyond appreciative of it. Shout out to the readers who have reached out to me to share your thoughts regarding my books. I thank you for keeping me motivated and excited to create new projects for you. When I write, I keep you in mind. Thank you for your support. It's my soul food.

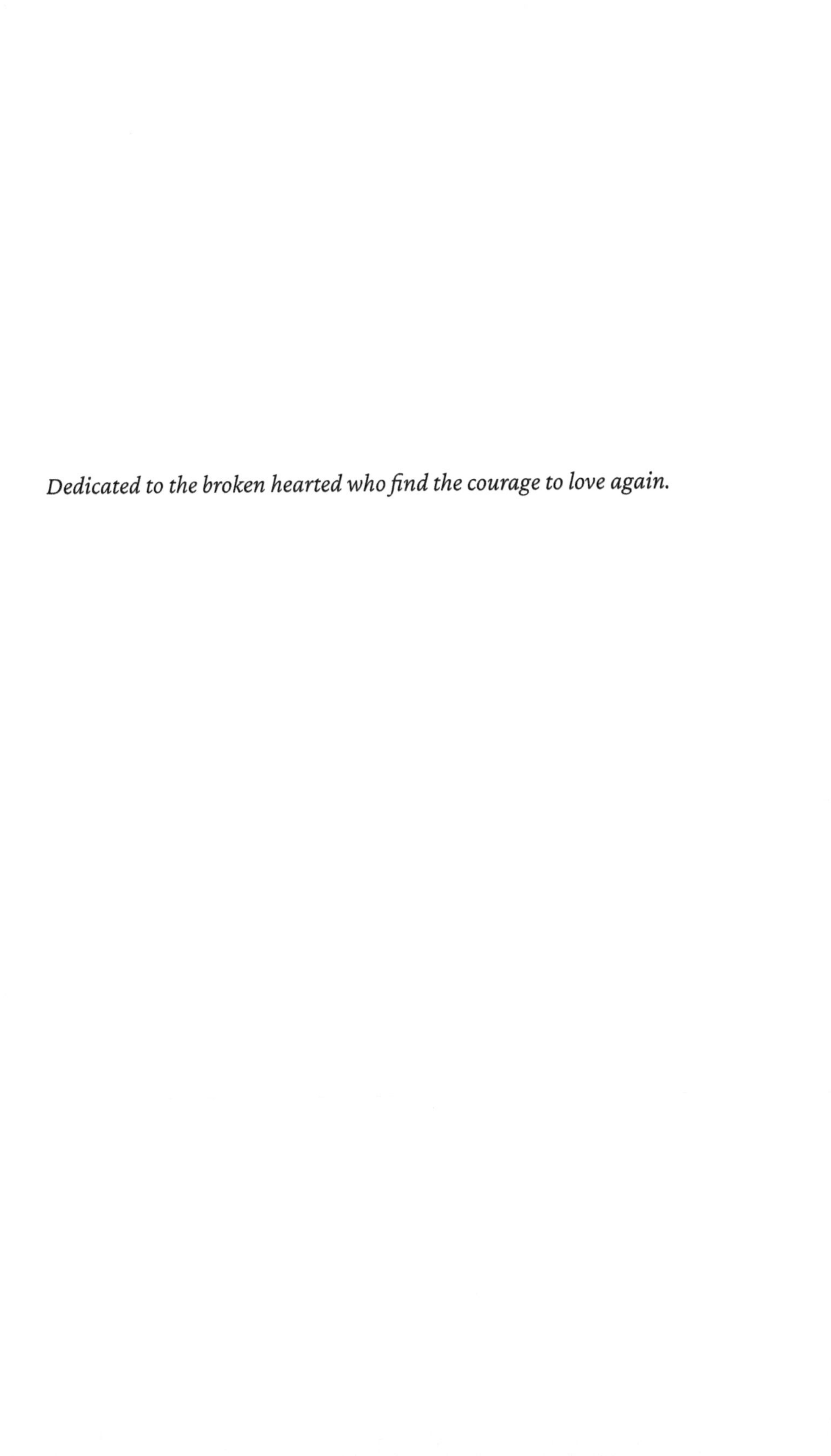

Dedicated to the broken hearted who find the courage to love again.

one

I ROLLED off my back and onto my right side, my arm extended for my iPhone. This was what I normally did first thing in the morning. Reach for my phone to check the time. It was the weekend, so the time wasn't a concern but still, time checks were my routine.

But when I stretched my hand, instead of feeling the edge of my night table, my fingers met nothing but air.

With eyes still closed, I grunted and raised my palm to my forehead to slap.

This meant only one thing. I wasn't home.

"Shit," I said as my eyes slowly peeled open.

I fell asleep on his bed at his apartment again.

"Stupid," I spat at myself, slapping my forehead a second time.

My focus settled on the ceiling before I pushed my elbows into the mattress to lift up. I shook my head and glanced to my left to see his spot temporarily empty.

"He didn't even bother to wake me up?" I asked out loud.

The *he* is Meki.

Yes, that Meki.

My next-door neighbor the asshole. The very sexy asshole with kissable lips, a body made for urban book covers, and who I've been allowing to sex me for over 12 months.

A whole damn year. Something that wasn't even supposed to happen had extended way past the limit of a hookup.

Don't judge me.

I sniffed the air and noticed the comforting aroma of coffee.

"Mmm." I sighed to myself. Some caffeine at that hour would be useful. My head felt light which meant the tequila shots I downed the night before still pulsed through my veins.

Intoxicated as hell was the best way to describe the last five or so hours. The aforementioned was typical whenever I spent the night with Meki. No, I wasn't drunk with him always, but drinking games had become our thing. Who could drink more? Hold their liquor better?

I kicked my legs off the mattress and grabbed his shirt that laid on the floor on my side of the bed.

I wasn't even supposed to be over there the night before. But boredom fueled by horniness struck me like lightning. So, I stepped out of my apartment, left my door unlocked, and knocked on his door, naked. Left all my clothes on my bed. I knew he'd get a kick out of it and I had no interest in sugarcoating the motive behind the visit. Sex influenced my arrival to his door... only sex.

A year.

A year of knocking on each other's doors, inviting one another in to do things lovers did when we didn't so much as care for each other.

After pulling his shirt that was three sizes too big over my head, I poked my arms through the short sleeves. I made my way to his closed bedroom door, opened it, and instantly heard his voice.

"So tomorrow night," I heard Meki say as I walked closer. "Do I really need to be in attendance?"

The moment I turned the corner and saw her I almost lost my footing.

The two sat at his kitchen table and glanced up at me. A smirk pulled at his lips as he leaned back in his seat and gave me his full attention.

"Good morning," he said, his focus on my legs as he bit his bottom lip.

I didn't even bother returning the greeting because I found it hard to believe who my eyes saw sitting beside him.

His mother.

"Josephine," I blurted.

Her name just rolled off my tongue and tumbled out my mouth. We never met until that moment, thank God. But it shocked the hell out of me to see her in his apartment.

Meki told me often how his mother limited her visits to his home. She considered the neighborhood to be too below her standards I guess. Well, that's what he told me.

I understood, and I didn't fault her for feeling that way.

Bushwick in Brooklyn wasn't everyone's first pick to live, but the area improved from decades past.

"Oh!" She blushed.

Josephine was beautiful. Gorgeous warm sepia skin, flowing light brown hair and eyes that sparkled. She looked a lot like Beverly Johnson with the height to match. She must've been close to 60-years-old but didn't appear a day over forty. Even seated I could tell she took good care of herself. And even in the twenty-degree weather New York had on that chilly Saturday morning in December, she kept her cleavage in full view.

"Have we met?" she asked.

My jaw dropped as her words found their way into my ears. Words accompanied by an accent.

"You're English?" I asked, managing to stop my jaw from hinging open. My eyes moved to Meki for answers. He snorted at my shock.

"So we haven't... met." Josephine smiled. Her smile was so picturesque, welcoming.

She likes me.

I refused to allow it.

"No, we haven't," I said. "And we shouldn't right now."

She turned her head to glance at Meki who chuckled in response.

"In fact," I added, walking backwards toward the front door to leave. "I'm not here. Let's pretend like I wasn't even here."

Josephine scratched her head. "Um..."

I turned to face the door.

"Darling?" Josephine cleared her throat. "You're not wearing any pants."

I glanced down at my bare thighs as if I wasn't already aware. "Oh, it's fine. I didn't come here with any clothes on last night. Plus, I'm just right there across the hall."

I reached for the doorknob. "It was nice meeting you... or not meeting you."

Meki burst out laughing.

As I pulled the door closed, he said, "See you later Cadence."

"Yeah, whatever," I mumbled, shutting the door behind myself.

* * *

An hour later, showered, and with pants on, I made my way out into my living room. The moment I sat on my couch and reached for the latest issue of Yoga Journal Magazine, I heard a light knock at my door.

I glanced at the door then at the digital clock on my cable box.

"Jehovah Witnesses," I said to myself. With that, I flipped open the magazine, prepared to ignore and peruse. But the knock came again.

"I'm not interested. Thank you," I said from the couch. "Go away."

"Cadence, it's Josephine."

I jerked my head back and furrowed my brows.

"Uh... oh... kay. One moment, please," I replied.

I did a quick scan of my place to make sure it looked descent. Having company when my apartment was a mess just wasn't my thing. But my place looked great. Thankfully, I straightened up that Friday, a routine. I loved routines. Saved me from moments like this. Needing to scramble, picking up this and that and for my place to still look like shit.

In front of my door, I pulled it open to see her standing on the other side with the same warm grin I left her with in Meki's apartment.

"Hi again," she said.

"Yeah, hi." I offered a cordial smile. "Did I leave something in Meki's apartment?"

"Yes," she answered. "An interesting first impression."

I bit back my laugh before briefly looking away.

Her eyes journeyed over my shoulder to inside of my home.

"Oh my," she said, pushing the door wider for a better view.

I had no choice but to step to the side when she crossed my threshold and stepped right past me.

I watched this woman invite herself in and couldn't find the words to stop her.

"Why don't you come inside?" I snarked.

She laughed. "I'm sorry darling. How rude was that? But my goodness..." She walked closer to the painting I had mounted to my wall between two windows. "Is this Basquiat?"

She was referring to the self-portrait of the late indie artist I purchased at a vintage art auction a few months back. I'd received a bonus at work and just as quick as the money landed in my bank account it waltzed right back out and into the hands of an indie art dealer.

"Yes." I beamed. "I'm broke because of it but, meh."

She giggled. "You're too cute."

I blushed in response.

The portrait was the one piece of art that added such class to my place. It hurt to part with that money but the rewards of seeing the Basquiat portrait every day was worth it. It gave my place a sophisti-cated urban touch. Plus, it was so me.

She turned to face me for only a moment before her eyes were back to visually digesting everything around herself. Her view moved from my tan couch to the solid gold figurines that lined the shelves nailed to my walls. The medium-sized bookcase shaped like the continent of Africa drew her closer where she peered at the spines of books stacked side-by-side.

"Your place is gorgeous Cadence, considering."

"Considering?" I asked.

"Well," she said removing her coat.

Dammit, she's getting comfortable. Great.

"This neighborhood is just not my cup of tea. But what you've done here is nothing short of magnificent."

Well, if she was looking to get on my good side she sure achieved it with her compliments.

With her coat off, I confirmed just how well Mrs. Knight cared for herself. She stood there donned in a simple black wrap dress that stressed her slim curves. With no need to ask, it was clear she worked out or at the very least ate right. I doubted Meki would have it any other way being a personal trainer and all.

"Bushwick has gotten better over the years." I folded my arms. "I apologize for being so forward, Mrs. Knight, but did you need something from me?"

"Mrs. Knight?" she challenged. "Darling, you've already referred to me as Josephine. You might as well continue to do so."

I dropped my view down to my feet to stop from smiling. "I'm sorry about that. I was just shocked to see you."

"Obviously. And yet you recognized me and knew my name without us ever having to meet. Does Meki speak of me often?"

"Sometimes," I replied. "But I recognized you from the research I've done. Google is an excellent resource."

She giggled. "I like you Cadence. You're full of spunk. You remind me of... me."

Comparison. It's true, she likes me. Maybe a little too much.

I closed my eyes and exhaled sharply. "Can I be honest with you, Josephine?"

"Of course."

"Although I am very flattered by your words, you liking me means very little."

She tilted her head to her right.

"How can I put this delicately? Umm... well, I can't. I don't like your son. At all."

"I'm sorry?" she queried.

"I mean, maybe I like him a little. But very little and not in the normal way. Sometimes I just cannot stand him."

She blinked in response but said nothing.

"I'm confused, dear. Were you not just in his apartment wearing no trousers?" she asked.

I snorted a laugh. "Yes, I was."

She wrinkled her brows while holding her stare with me.

"What Meki and I have is... really just... well, physical."

She twisted her mouth to one side.

"It's just sex," I blurted.

Her brows suddenly arched. "Oh!"

"So," I continued, "you liking me is not something I care for at the moment or ever. Considering the relationship your son and I have. Which isn't a relationship at all? It really is just sex between us. Nothing more, nothing less."

"Wow," she said, scrubbing the middle of her forehead with her fingertips. "I don't think I've ever heard that before. Every woman who has ever fancied my Meki found themselves infatuated with him."

"Well," I said, shrugging my shoulders, "there's a first time for everything, right?"

"Right." She smiled.

Josephine stood quiet for a moment, holding her smile with me and the silence made things awkward.

"So... um..."

"Listen," she interjected before I had the chance to continue, "I'm having a New Year's Eve gala, tomorrow night starting at 7 p.m. I want you to be there."

Oh, hell yeah!

Okay, now, Meki I couldn't care less for but Josephine Knight's galas I would give my right arm to attend. Her galas, from my research, were one of the hottest tickets in town. Everyone who was anyone attended every single one. Celebrities, politicians, the crème de la crème of black entrepreneurs. It was the place to be. And for someone like myself who was broke but liked being around money, the invitation was something I had to accept.

"Okay... but just as a guest right? Nothing more?"

She smiled then giggled. "Only as a guest."

Josephine picked up her coat and held it out for me to take. "Do you mind, darling?"

I accepted her YSL wool pea coat and smiled, admiring the cut as I held it opened behind her so she had room to glide her arms through the sleeves.

"Nice coat," I told her.

"YSL," she said as she shrugged it over her shoulders.

As if I didn't already check the label.

"So," she said making her way over to my door and pulling it open. "Tomorrow night at 7 p.m. wear your best and come prepared to mingle. It'll be a night to remember."

"I'm sure," I said. "Thank you, Mrs. Knight."

She stepped into the hallway, turned and pointed at me.

"I mean, Josephine."

She winked and made her way down the stairs.

A night with the Knights.

This would be interesting.

Unbeknown to me, the next night would set off a series of events that would change my life and my relationship or lack thereof with Meki forever.

two

I ARRIVED at the Knight's estate at 7 p.m. on the dot. Timed my arrival before leaving my apartment and scheduling a black car to pick me up from in front of the building. I hated being late. I considered it to be a sign of disrespect. Although people of color were the main ones to attend the event, this was the top tier elite crew. They weren't down with being fashionably late despite the misconception.

A winding road and a plethora of windows is the best way to describe outside the Knight's property. Pruned bushes and well-manicured trees slowly came into view as my driver drove closer to the front doors of the mansion.

In Southampton on the very exclusive Old Towne Lane, the Knight Estate was a three-story 15,500 square foot property out in Long Island.

There was no way I would roll through here just wearing something out of my closet. That would be uncivilized. So I did the most logical thing; I maxed out two credit cards for the Marchesa crimson red gown with a split so high it would make a stripper blush. Fresh pressed hair, a light application of foundation, and bold rouge lips completed the look.

I served face, body, and class that night. It was required. Josephine said for me to come prepared to mingle.

The moment I approached the entrance, a tuxedo-donned gentleman with creamy brown skin, extended his hand with a tray filled with glasses of champagne.

"Welcome," he greeted. "May I offer you a glass of champagne?"

I smiled from ear-to-ear. "You most certainly can."

Inside the mansion, my jaw dropped at the high ceilings and detailed crown moldings. Uniformed attendants guided me through the doors of the grand foyer where all the guests stood below me and across from each other sipping on champagne while socializing. They were all so beautiful and shined like they took showers in a different kind of water. The type of water imported from the nonexistent fountains on mars. There was a certain glow to people who had extra zeros in their bank accounts. At least they appeared that way.

The moment I stepped closer to one of the two banisters that extended down in opposite directions along winding staircases leading to the grand ballroom, my eyes met Meki's. The Knights had a damn ballroom on their property. Large and cinematic, and Meki stood out like a movie star among scene extras.

"Mmm," I moaned to myself. One thing I had to give the man, he was beautiful. Uniquely sexy with the right amount of God quality while appearing like only a man.

Normally, Meki didn't pay much attention to his appearance. He always kept himself groomed properly, and he wore the best outfits but they were often gym attire. You know, sweat pants, tee shirts, sneakers, hooded sweaters... stuff like that.

But that night, he dressed himself to perfection. Tailored black tuxedo with a bow tie to match. The tux fit him well, it did a great job stressing the contour of his ripped arms.

He saw me the moment I saw him and just us looking at each other drew us closer like magnets.

Crazy how in a room full of people, sexual energy can travel and no one be the wiser.

As I made my way down the stairs, he pulled himself away from a conversation he held with a woman and made his way over.

We met a few feet away at the bottom of those stairs. When he was close, he approached slow like a lion on the prowl. Then he walked around me twice causing goosebumps to freckle my skin. On his second go round, I inhaled the surrounding air.

He has on cologne, dammit.

Meki smelled like a walking orgasm waiting to happen.

"Not this dress," he said in my ear.

This dress cost me close to two grand but it was worth it. A last minute buy that gave the impression the makers of this dress had been working on the perfect fit for months and with only me in mind. My cleavage sat just right, and the fabric was like stretched silk. It was marvelous.

"You like?" I asked him, taking a sip of my champagne.

He stopped in front of me and briefly bent his legs at the knees long enough for us to be eye-to-eye for a moment. "Do I like?"

I giggled.

"No, I love." Meki glanced over his shoulder and moved in closer. He stood so close, only air could pass between us. "You know what I'd love even more?"

"What?" I asked, looking in his eyes.

"Just how good it's gonna lay wrinkled on my bedroom floor."

I laughed. "You always say that."

"Because I mean it."

I stared in his eyes and saw that fire. Fire often accompanied by the act that caused me to fall asleep in his bed once it was finally extinguished.

"Let's take a trip to the bathroom," he told me.

"Whatever you have to tell me in there you're more than welcome to tell me out here."

"Oh I'm sorry. Did I say we would talk in there?"

I pushed him away, and he laughed.

"Meki," a woman said behind him. When he stepped to the side, I got a better view of her.

Long, straight dark hair, umber-brown complexion, tall with piercing eyes that stared through me the whole time she walked closer. "Why did you walk away like that?"

She was the woman Meki spoke to before he saw me and left her standing at the bar.

I smiled politely, and she refused to return one back. She said nothing, so I figured I'd speak first.

"Hi. I'm Cadence Nice," I said, my hand extended. Normally I wouldn't bother but this event only had the best of the best in attendance. Couldn't give the attitude I usually would for people like herself.

"Giselle Menard. Charmed." She reached her hand out for me to take, palms down, fingers directed at the floor. I accepted then released her hand as quick as I could. Her hand was cold, like her presence.

"Nice," she said, her eyes pointing up at the high ceiling. "I don't think I've heard that surname before tonight. What family are you a part of?"

Meki cleared his throat. "Cadence isn't a part of the colored aristocrats."

The colored aristocrats, a.k.a. the black elite, were the families with old money. A group of well-off black people born with silver spoons already waiting for their mouths. This was all thanks to the wealth their ancestors built eons ago. Wealth maintained in the family name through companies that focused on real estate, engineering, medicine, catering, and other businesses.

"Oh," she said looking me up and down. "Nice dress Ms. Nice."

I offered a chuckle then turned away. I was putting in overtime keeping my eyes from rolling.

"So, if she isn't associated with any of the families," she said moving her eyes off Meki and back on me. "How did she get in here?"

"Josephine invited me."

And right on cue, I spotted Meki's mother offering kisses and hugs to the people she passed as she made her way closer to our huddle. The woman walked like she floated through the crowd. So graceful.

"Josephine?" Giselle quizzed. "You mean, Mrs. Knight?"

"I love when I'm already being spoken of before I join a conversation," Josephine said as she approached. "Cadence!"

She placed her hands on either side of my shoulders, pulled me close and gave me two air kisses, one on each cheek. "You came! And my goodness, this dress."

Josephine stepped back to get a better view of me. "Marchesa?"

My cheeks dimpled from the huge smile I allowed to pull at my lips. I was happy she noticed. Not sure why that even mattered. But it did. "Wow, how did you know?"

"Darling." She blushed. "I'm very good friends with Georgina and Karen. Attended their runway show earlier this year. I'll inform them that their latest creation is in good hands."

Josephine looked phenomenal herself. Dressed in a white gown with a pronounced ruched off the shoulder design.

"You look gorgeous," I told her.

"Don't I know it?" Josephine did a quick twirl, adjusting the tail of her dress accordingly.

"Yes, Josephine. Stunning," Giselle chimed in.

Meki chuckled softly.

"Oh, no, no, love. You can call me Mrs. Knight," Josephine said to Giselle.

I tucked my lips into my mouth to keep from laughing.

"We put out a new tray of croquettes." Josephine pointed. "Giselle, dear, help yourself to some. I saw you sip on one too many flutes of champagne. You need to soak it up with something."

Giselle blinked her response and nodded. "I always love having your croquettes. The best in New York."

Josephine smiled politely and held her view with Giselle until Giselle excused herself then walked away.

Giselle peeked over her shoulder at me with squared eyes as she left.

"Well," Josephine said, turning to face Meki and I. "God, you two pair up perfectly"

Meki and I glanced at each other and I released a shaky sigh.

I said to her, "Only as a guest, right?"

"Honestly, Cadence," she said walking up to Meki. She adjusted the direction of his bow tie and he allowed it by lifting his chin to give her more room to work. I thought the gesture was cute. "My fingers were crossed when I told you that."

I laughed.

"Meki," Josephine said. "Why don't you show Cadence around the property? There is a lot to see and I'm sure someone who loves the aesthetics like herself will appreciate a tour."

"Aight, I can do that."

Josephine cringed. "Meki." She rolled her eyes. "The street slang, sweetheart, must you?"

Meki snickered and so did I.

She ran her fingers through her hair and flashed us a winning smile. "Go on. See you two in a few."

* * *

The buzz of chatter dissipated the farther into the mansion Meki and I walked. The Knight Estate was beyond massive. I thought it was big from outside but inside was like the size of a tiny country. Ten bedrooms, and fourteen and a half bathrooms. Meki's old humble abode was the largest property I'd ever toured. I would bet money his parents' mansion was bigger than Brooklyn's Kings Plaza mall... with the parking lot attached.

"Wow." I gazed up above us. In the foyer that led away from the grand ballroom was a star-painted ceiling that reminded me of the ceiling in Manhattan's Grand Central Terminal. "That's beautiful."

"My mother has a love for the arts like someone I know."

All it took was feeling the clasp of his hand around mine for me to become tensed. I glanced down to see him trying to interlock his fingers with mine.

I pulled away instantly.

"What are you doing?" I asked, forcing a space between us. I stopped walking and turned to face him. He moved in closer.

Meki licked his lips as he took my hand again, guiding me against one of the hallway walls. I turned my head from left to right, checking both sides of the hall.

"I'm giving you a tour."

He smiled, no smirked, at me and I rolled my eyes pushing him back.

I quickly stepped away from the wall.

"What's this way?" I pointed up the hall and to the right.

"The bowling alley and theater." Meki walked up behind me and wrapped his arms around my waist.

"You have a bowling alley and a movie theater in here?"

Meki moved my hair off my shoulder and swooped it to the other shoulder before placing a kiss there. "Mm-hmm."

I shrugged him off me. "Can you stop that?"

"Really?" He shook his head. "You can't honestly expect for me to behave myself when you have this on." His fingers traveled down the side of my hip and I couldn't help the shiver he caused from his touch.

This... this thing he did. A thing that got me to do whatever he wanted and that I identified as being a weakness, I always anticipated giving in to. How pathetic right?

"What else does this place have?"

He kissed his teeth. "Come on Cadence. You really care that much about my parents' mansion? It's not that amazing, trust me."

"Your mother told you to give me a tour."

"I know what she told me but I had no intentions of doing that. Now get over here with your sexy ass."

I put my hands up between us and he removed them quick.

"Stop playing hard to get," he whispered.

"I'm not playing," I shot back, looking up in his eyes.

He smiled and said, "Touché."

"Why didn't you tell me your mother was English?"

I didn't really care but a part of me was curious. We'd known each other for a year. Meki and I didn't speak much about our families. Our conversations weren't about anything personal. Other than cluing one another in on when we were free to have sex, everything was just physical between us. But I wondered why he never shared that tidbit of info when discussing his mother.

"She isn't," he said stepping back. "Technically she isn't. Let's check out my room."

Meki and I made our way down the corridor. We passed by the door that led to the pool and pool house, his staffs' bedrooms, and stopped at the estate's elevator.

We rode that elevator to the top floor and stepped out into another wing of the house that appeared different from the one where the party was being held.

This part of the mansion had all the makings of a home. Photos of the family lined the walls in a geometric style that looked fancy but humble.

"What do you mean she isn't English? She has an accent."

"She was born in DC but moved to Europe before she was old enough to walk. My grandparents had business out there. Business ended up being better than they expected so they set up shop and a home in England. They didn't return to the states until my mother was fourteen and she's been here ever since. She has dual citizenship though."

"Hmph, impressive."

"This way," he said pointing ahead of us.

We approached one of the tall mahogany doors when Meki reached for the knob and turned to glance at me over his shoulder.

"Ready?"

"Just open it," I sassed.

The moment the door opened, I walked into a room that looked like a place Meki wouldn't call his own.

A large work desk pushed up against the wall, a bed with designer bedding hugging the mattress. A simple fireplace and Oakwood paneling finished the basic yet elegant bedroom.

"Exquisite," I said, walking farther into the room. "This looks nothing like you."

"You're right, it doesn't. It looks like my parents."

Meki shut the door and leaned his back against it, staring at me.

"What?"

"Nothing," he said, pushing himself off the door and heading my way slow. "You look good in here."

I rolled my eyes, my lips tight as I tried my hardest to fight back my smile.

"Oh please, I see you blushing over there."

I rolled my eyes again, and this time shook my head too.

"When are we going to stop playing this silly game of who dislikes who more?"

"The only time you're even remotely polite, Meki, is when you want someplace wet and warm to bury your hard-on."

He laughed. "Crass much?"

"I'm just keeping it real."

"Well, I could say the same about you. Only pleasant when you want a release."

Meki stood in front of me, pushing his hands into his pockets. He glided his eyes down my form, licking his lips at every curve he gawked at on me.

He pointed his chin at my cleavage and said, "Take that off for me."

I scoffed.

"Will you please take it off?"

"Will you beg me?" I challenged.

He grinned. "Do you want me to beg you?"

"Maybe."

Meki moved behind me and his presence sent a chill down my spine.

"You already know I don't beg. Ever," he said in my ear. I felt the tips of his fingers glide up my back to the top of my zipper.

"I'm not about to sleep with you in your parents' mansion," I said to him low.

"Oh, don't worry..." The hiss of my zipper coming undone as he unzipped it replaced his words. "We won't be getting any sleep here, at all. That I can promise you."

"Meki—"

"Tell me you don't want me right now, Cae."

He turned me to face him then walked me against the wall behind us. There, Meki peeled the straps of my dress down my shoulders, revealing my strapless nude-colored bra I wore underneath.

"Fine," I said as I looked away, "I don't want you right now."

"No." He turned my head by my chin. "Look me in the eyes and tell me that lie."

I released my exhale through my mouth.

He loosened his bow tie, removing it and dropping it to the floor beneath our feet. Then he unbuttoned his shirt until that shirt laid at his chest, opened, revealing his tatted peck and sculpted abs too.

I turned my face away from his and he turned it back. I shoved him and he grabbed my wrists and cuffed them above my head.

The moan I'd been holding in, hummed from my mouth and the reaction made him grin.

He closed the space between us and brought his lips to my neck. The feel of his mouth and warm breath against my skin made my nipples tight.

"I wanna see your face as you lie to me," he whispered on my neck. Meki left a single kiss on that spot and that little kiss made my walls pulse.

"Just do it."

"Do what?"

I sighed. "It."

"Beg me," he countered.

I pursed my lips.

"Beg," he ordered.

I stared at him and he stared back.

He arched a brow signaling for me to comply.

Finally, I whispered, "Please do it."

"Please do what? Be specific."

I rolled my eyes. "You know what."

"But I want to hear you say it."

I fought back my smile by holding my lips tight.

He smirked in response. "I'm waiting."

"Fuck me."

"Yeah," he said nodding, "You have no idea how much I love when you talk like that."

Meki bit his thick bottom lip and turned me around to face the wall. His hands gripped the side of my dress as he rolled the fabric up my thighs.

Once over my hips, he hooked the sides of my panties with his fingers and slid them down to my knees.

The crinkling sound the condom made behind me was like an auditory aphrodisiac.

"Don't make me wait too long," I said, dropping my head between my shoulders.

Meki leaned close. In my ear he replied, "Never."

He pressed one hand against the wall in front of me and used the other to pull me closer using my right hip.

His first upstroke almost made me climb that wall. The strokes he delivered after that were in rhythm and synchronized with his moans. Like he was moving to a silent beat. Creating the perfect song.

I tried to keep my moans to myself but what was the use? Whenever we let our bodies talk, I refused to suppress my delight.

The sound of our skin meeting, my ass clapping against him sent the results of the act soon surging through my body.

Meki's hand crept up to my throat where he gripped my neck. He brought his mouth to my right ear and sucked on my earlobe.

I moaned my gratitude up at the bedroom's ceiling, my voice the only voice traveling around us.

"Oh God, don't stop." I pleaded. "I'm coming."

"You know the deal, Cae," he exhaled in my ear. "Ask me for my permission first."

I smiled at the request.

Sometimes I obeyed, often times I didn't since I understood how much he hated me challenging him. But ignoring his orders had its perks.

"May I?"

"No. You can wait."

"You know I never can."

He moaned in response. "Come for me then."

The next thing I felt was the slap of his palm against my ass before he palmed it.

I yelped, and he slowed his pace.

"Too hard?"

"Mmm," I moaned. "Not hard enough."

"Good girl." He growled. "That's what I like to hear."

three

FORTY-SEVEN MINUTES later Meki and I returned to the party. I excused myself to step into the bathroom since there was no way I'd return to the gala smelling like sex.

I'd be lying if I said I didn't enjoy that little thing we did up in his room. How he understood my body well enough to make me climax on command. It baffled me how he understood what to say to bring me to a place of physical nirvana.

Tucked in a corner and near the grand ballroom was a powder room that doubled as a bathroom. Only three stalls made up the space but inside was empty when I stepped in through the door.

After handling my business, I reached for the latch to unlock the door but paused when chatter grew closer.

"I cannot believe she is what he's into, Penelope," the woman said.

"Neither can I. What was her name again?" Penelope asked.

"Cadence," the woman spat.

Instantly I knew who it was.

I peered through the gap at the side of the stall door, watching as the two women spoke of me. Giselle was one-half of the converser.

"Well, at least her parents gave her a pretty name," Penelope said.

"Hmph, did they?" Giselle questioned, flipping her hair over her shoulder and leaning over the vanity table to check her makeup in the mirror. "The name is as basic as the person wearing it. And speaking of wearing... did you see her dress?"

"Well, now, her dress is beautiful." Penelope admitted. "Can't say anything against that."

I smiled to myself.

Giselle looked over at Penelope and sneered before turning away. "It's not that impressive. I'm sure she picked the dress up at Neiman Marcus right off the rack, Penelope. With her broke ass."

I balled my hands into fists.

Penelope shrugged.

"And even if the dress *were* beautiful... let's be honest, it's the dress that has Meki all heart-eyed and smitten. Without it I'm sure little Ms. Brooklyn is just as regular as they come."

"Brooklyn, is that where she lives?" Penelope asked. "Eww."

"I know right?" Giselle said next, pressing her hand to her chest with a look of disgust on her face. "I can't understand why Meki insisted on leaving this palace to go be among paupers like her. Ms. Nice must be the nice petite whore he desires. In a few months' time he'll be over her and will move on to better things. Like moi. I will cleanse all that ghetto shit out of him when he does."

I slid the latch off the stall door quick and stepped out.

Penelope gasped and Giselle did a double take when they saw me standing there behind them.

I walked over to the vanity counter where they stood. Turned on the faucet in the sink and rinsed my hands before leaning in Giselle's direction to access the soap dispenser.

She quickly moved out of the way.

They said nothing the whole time I stood right beside them. Typical. Got all that shit to say about me but not a damn thing to say to me.

After drying my hands I decided to shatter the silence.

"For the record, ladies," I said, staring at my reflection in the mirror over the vanity. "It's not the dress that's got Meki so enamored."

Giselle swallowed hard.

"In fact, he can't wait to get me out of it." I walked closer and Giselle stepped backwards. "What I have that's got him hooked, you can't find in stores. It's limited edition. Only one of its kind. And it's called... me. Sorry to disappoint."

I turned to leave the bathroom and as I left, I added, "And he and I have been seeing each other for well over a year, Giselle. Done, is the furthest thing he is with me."

I didn't even look back at them to read their faces as I allowed the bathroom door to close behind me.

* * *

A few days later I was back at work in my office typing up emails and double checking schedules. I liked my job and the people I worked with. Being employed by a forward thinking company with a young employee culture made things delightful. And corporate life continued to improve with time.

I'd moved up in the firm and there had been whispers I'd be climbing the corporate ladder yet again.

That night at the gala, after checking the bitch and her minion in the bathroom, I returned to the party. I got a chance to meet Meki's father and Meki's two older brothers, Braxton and Alexander. His brothers were nothing like Meki. Well-mannered and preppy looking. Braxton kept calling me Candace which only bothered me after I returned home and it plagued my mind.

Meki Knight, Sr, was a soft-spoken gentleman who managed to be at the party but not there the entire night. Meki would later reveal the galas weren't his father's thing but his dad took part in them because he understood how much Josephine loved hosting them.

"Why'd your parents give you your father's name?" I asked Meki as we wrestled with removing our clothes back at my place that same night. We always required two rounds.

"What?" he exhaled, kissing me on my neck.

"Your name. Why are you your father's junior? Why wouldn't one of your older brothers get his name instead?"

Meki stepped back for a moment to meet my eyes. "You're asking me this now?" He grabbed my hand and placed it on his hard-on to hold. "Do you feel this? Do you really think this is the conversation I want to have right now?"

I wrapped my hands around his shaft and he groaned at the feeling.

"I'm just curious."

He lifted me in his arms and dropped me on the bed, peeling his shirt down his biceps.

"I was a mistake and they couldn't think of any other name to give me," he said, before pulling me to the edge of the bed and closer to him using just my legs.

His words echoed in my mind the rest of the night and for the past few days after. No one confessed to being "a mistake." I left the discussion alone though. Diving any more into conversation would hint I cared, and I didn't.

Giselle avoided me for the remainder of the night at the gala. Why wouldn't she? She must've felt embarrassed after getting caught in the bathroom caught up in her jealous tirade armed with insults.

It was whatever. I'd be lying if I said it didn't hurt a little hearing her talk about me like that. But just like the soap I washed my hands with, I understood envy lathered most of her words. If a man like Meki paid that much attention to someone other than me, I'd be just as salty.

It was my first day back at work, everyone's first day. York Integrations, the IT firm I worked at, liked to give two extra paid-days off after New Year's Day. According to management, the extended break was good for company moral. I appreciated the opportunity to rest.

We'd only just started the day when I heard a bunch of commotion outside my office door.

I straightened my blazer and smoothed down my pencil skirt as I made my way around my desk and out my door.

"Oh my God, Simone, congratulations!" one of my coworkers gushed. "And that ring is everything."

I stood at the threshold of my door watching as Simone beamed from ear-to-ear. Her hand extended in every which way showing off the sizable rock on her ring finger.

I forced a smile but deep down I couldn't care less.

"Isn't it beautiful?" Olivia, my office manager, asked as she joined me at my door.

"It is," I lied. I couldn't really see the ring but I wasn't about to act like I didn't care.

Office politics.

"She and her fiancé were together for like twelve years. I don't know if I could've waited that long."

I smiled politely not at all interested in adding to her thought.

Everyone at work knew I was in a relationship with my ex-boyfriend Terrell for close to that long. When we broke up, I never made an announcement. Everyone figured things didn't work out between us when I told them I was moving into my apartment alone a year ago.

"Been there. Not again," I mumbled.

"I hear that." Olivia giggled. "I'll see you at lunch."

I stood at my doorway watching Simone as she moved from cubicle to cubicle, her hand leading the way. Other coworkers gripped her fingers and brought their smiling eyes closer to her diamond as if the ring had magical powers. Like gawking at the diamond's pear-shape long enough would manifest something similar in their lives.

"Dare to dream, ladies. Aspire higher," I said to myself before returning to my office and closing the door.

26

four

THE IMPACT of the asphalt beneath my feet sent a wave of motion up my calves, vibrating throughout my thighs. I pulled in cold air through my mouth and released it the same way, my heart mimicking the sound of a jackhammer, trying to keep up with my movements. My breaths were even though, steady. It took time to master that, along with my runner's pace.

I ran alongside Meki as we jogged through Brooklyn's Prospect Park. The harsh wind felt like ice when I inhaled it through my nose earlier in our run, so I passed on doing that. Plus, breathing in and out through my mouth helped me keep up with Meki who excelled at running the parks.

My lungs burned, but I wouldn't show that. Not with that man running alongside me. He ran for just as long as I did but you wouldn't be able to tell by the smirk he wore on his lips.

"Come on, Cadence," he exhaled. He peered at me from the side of his gray hood he kept over his head. He ran up ahead of me and said, "You've got to add a little more speed baby. You're slowing me down out here."

More speed? Seriously?! I'm barely hanging on.

"Oh whatever. You look like you're having trouble keeping up with me."

He let a sexy laugh bellow from his mouth then reached over to slap me on the ass.

"Hey!" I yelled.

He turned on his heels and ran backwards, maintaining the same pace and offering a condescending grin.

"You're such a fucking showoff," I spat.

"You love it."

"Yeah, okay."

We ran for another half a mile then decided to take a break. Well, he offered to take a break, and I obliged because really, I couldn't take anymore.

In the summer, Brooklyn's Prospect Park was scenic. After all the renovating and work they did on the park, it had become a sight to see. A myriad of trees framed the landscape. In the winter, the trees were bare, like thin arms reaching out to the sun above for warmth. Barely any grass along the lawns. Old man winter sucked the park dry of all the beauty it had for the season.

Meki pointed. "Let's stretch in the gazebo."

Running with Meki had become a routine of mine. Most Saturday mornings, he'd knock on my door and suggest we drive out to the park for a run. Yoga was my exercise of choice, but I didn't work up a sweat the way I did with running. So I never declined his invite to join him.

Meki was the top trainer at Robert Kurt's gym in the city. Meki trained celebrities like actors and models and understood how to sculpt bodies. Sessions with Meki cost upwards of one hundred thousand a year. The fee for access to the gym, without a trainer, was close to a grand a month. Hell, just a day pass was four hundred dollars. So, I never refused an invitation to workout with one of the best. I never told him I considered him to be one of the best though. His ego was way too big, and I believed just a single compliment might make his head explode. But he was the best at just about everything. Especially in matters of satisfying my body.

"Lay on your back," he said pointing at the gazebo's boarded floors.

Meki insisted we stretch before and after our workouts. And for the year we'd been running together, I've never been sore after a run with him. Gentle and effective, his hands on me always provided me with comfort. I had to work overtime not to show that though.

"You lasted longer today," he told me as he lifted my right leg and moved my foot in a circle. "Your stamina has improved. Have you noticed?"

"I've always had good stamina Meki but thanks."

He snickered. "I beg to differ. Sit up and lean forward."

Meki moved behind me, pressing his thumbs to my lower back and pushing the pad of his fingers into my spine.

"Were you really a mistake?" I asked in my forward fold.

"What?"

"That night at my place after your mother's New Year's Eve gala. I asked you why your parents gave you your father's name and not your older brothers and you told me your parents named you after your dad because you were a mistake."

"Would you have sympathy for me if I confirmed that?" he asked.

I shrugged. "I mean... I really don't care."

"As always. Lay back down on your back."

He walked in front of me and lifted my left leg, doing the same stretching motions as he did with my right. "You're always telling me you don't care but the questions you ask proves otherwise."

"Hmph." I peered up in his eyes and he smiled at me.

So damn handsome.

"I wasn't planned like my two older brothers. My parents thought they were done making and having kids after my mother gave birth to my brother Alexander. My father even arranged to get a vasectomy a month before my mother got pregnant with me."

I blinked in response, hoping he'd continue.

"So, when they found out she was pregnant, my father took that as a sign to pass along his name. Continue the family legacy since his father and his father's father maintained the names and surnames. He refused to do that with my older brothers because he wanted them to have their own identities. Personally, I think my parents just didn't want to go through the hassle of deciding on a name. So they went with what worked."

"That's flattering."

"It's whatever." He shrugged, his focus my thighs.

Meki glided his hands down my legs, only stopping when he grazed the V indentation between my thighs.

He looked up and in my eyes.

Expecting to see the usual lustful look, I saw something else. Something softer, more intimate.

His stare made me do a double take. That's because it was more of a gaze, his eyes dancing along my face, examining my features like he was saving it to memory for later thoughts of me. A small smile pulled at his lips and he took a deep breath in and released it slow.

My brows creased. "What?"

He broke focus at once. "Nothing," he said, clearing his throat and blinking repeatedly. Like he attempted to blink himself out of a moment. "You're good now."

Meki was on his feet as he sat back, balancing himself on the arch of his foot while extending his right leg to the side of himself.

What the hell was that?

The man looked lost in my eyes. Like someone... in love.

Naaaa, no way.

Right?

five

THE FOLLOWING MONTH, three days into February, my mother invited my cousin and I over for dinner. My mother, Corrine Stewart, was my first best friend ever. I could speak with her about everything... well, not everything. She had no idea Meki, and I were seeing each other. She wasn't even aware of his existence, and I intended to keep it that way.

My mother was traditional even though she had an untraditional past. Baby out of wedlock and only married after being in an on-and-off-again relationship with my step-father, Ronald Waters, for close to two decades.

She and Ronald, I call him pops, finally tied the knot after my eighteenth birthday. Still, if I told her I was in a casual sex arrangement with a man I didn't care for, she'd clutch her pearls and paint a red A on my chest.

My cousin Caira never passed up an opportunity to grub at my mother's home.

In Newark, New Jersey, the townhouse was where I spent most of my life before I ran off to college. The neighborhood I grew up in wasn't the best but it didn't qualify as the worst either.

Our house was a small three-bedroom home with a tiny kitchen and a tinier bathroom but it worked. My mother did an excellent job making the house feel like a home.

More photos of me, lined the walls and surfaces of the living area.

No matter the decade, my mother refused to remove the carpets she had in every room. I told her everyone chose hardwood floors these days, but she's a creature of habit. She likes what she likes.

My mother and step-father have lived here in this home, on this block, long enough where everyone knew their names so no one messed with them.

"Y'all go ahead and hang out for a bit. The food will be ready in half an hour," my mother said the moment Caira, and I walked through the door.

We'd just stepped in the house moments after pulling up at the curb in Caira's car.

"It smells great in here, aunty. Good thing I came here hungry." Caira smiled.

"As always." My mother laughed. "And I don't see where the food goes once you put it in your mouth because you still thin like a wire hanger."

"It's all the sex I have," Caira said under her breath, low for only me to hear. She nudged me on the shoulder and giggled.

"What did you say little girl?" My mother asked. "Speak up."

Caira didn't say it low enough.

"Nothing." Caira pushed me up the stairs in front of her. "We'll be upstairs."

"Mm-hmm... that's what I thought."

I laughed to myself.

Along the way my eyes met photos of me from my younger years, nailed to the wall beside the stairs that led the way upstairs.

"Hey, pops," I said to my step-father, Ronald, as Caira and I passed by he and my mother's bedroom. He laid reclined on the bed, his back against the headboard, eyes glued to the basketball game on the TV in front of him.

"Hey there, baby girl," he replied, his eyes still on the screen.

"Hey Uncle Ronald," Caira said next. "Who's winning?"

"Damn Cavaliers," he spat. "I don't understand why every year these Knicks keep losing. Shit! I got a hundred riding on this game."

"Now, pops, that's your fault," I teased. "You were better off betting on the Cavaliers. I'm sure all the other Knicks fans did."

"Hmph. If I wasn't so tired, I'd get up and close that door," he mumbled.

Caira and I looked at each other and giggled.

My mother and step-father had been together since I was about 4-years-old... on and off again. But even when my step-father and mother weren't on good terms, he always maintained his relationship with me.

Although my biological father was in my life, we'd speak on holidays and other random occasions when I crossed his mind, my bond with Ronald was stronger. I always considered him to be more of a father than my dad. Ronald bought me my first car, footed part of the bill for my education, and grilled every boy who had the balls to call our home phone or show up on our doorstep. Ronald, to me, was my real dad.

Caira and I made our way into my room when she closed the door behind herself.

"You almost got popped on the mouth for that sly comment you made downstairs, huh? Acting like you weren't aware the woman has dog ears," I joked.

Caira laughed. "I would've repeated myself if I wasn't so hungry. I'm not trying to get put out before dinner."

Caira.

My cousin was still just as crazy as she was when we were younger. I considered her to be my best friend, my ace, my partner in crime. And she was a bad influence, influence I did well not to follow.

"You lookin' a little thick in the hips there, cuzzo," Caira said slapping me on my thigh. "Putting on relationship weight, huh?"

"What?!" I shrieked, jumping to my feet and walking to my

mirror that hung over my bedroom door. "I haven't put on a pound of relationship weight. What are you talking about? I'm not even in a relationship."

Caira laughed. "So what do you call this thing you got going on with Meki then?"

"Sex."

"Okay, but you've only been having sex with him."

"So?" I shrugged. "That doesn't make us a couple."

"Oh no? So who else is he fucking?"

I pointed my eyes up at the ceiling. "No one that I know of, but—"

"So you're not sexing anyone else and neither is he. You both call one another when you want it and go out together from time to time."

"To run in parks."

She pursed her lips. "Cadence please. You two have gone out to eat too, stop lying."

"To nowhere fancy, and that's only because we're hungry. That's not even worth mentioning. It's not like a date or anything," I said. "We don't even like each other like that. We got that one connection."

"But you both are seeing and connecting with no one else, right?"

"No, we're not."

She laughed out loud.

"Bitch," Caira said through her laughs. "You're in a relationship."

I rolled my eyes and dropped myself onto my bed as she continued giggling.

"Look, Cadence, it's fine." She placed a hand on my shoulder. "Y'all are exclusive. You two just have said nothing about it. That's cool."

"No." I sat up. "We are not exclusive. I could go on a date with anyone else, have sex with someone other than Meki and it'll be whatever to him. And the same applies to me."

Caira shook her head. "You're in denial."

"I am not."

"I'm sure finding a second fuck buddy isn't a challenge for the man. Not in the least. Meki is a really handsome man, Cadence. You don't need me to tell you that. He can have any woman he wants. Hell, even I would let him hit knowing he has a girl but you're my cousin so that makes him completely off limits."

I shoved her, and she laughed.

"You little ho. And I am not his girl, Caira."

"But I'm sayin'..."

"Caira, you're looking too much into this." I stood up from my spot on the bed and walked over to my window, peeling back the curtain and glimpsing an elderly couple sitting on their stoop holding hands. "What Meki and I have is nothing more than just sex."

"And yet, you visited his family's home for a party."

"That his mother invited me to attend."

"Which you accepted."

I rolled my eyes.

"And the way you described it... how she was all like, give her a tour Meki, show her around Meki, tells me Meki's mother likes you, maybe even more than he does."

"I'm not looking for all that." I turned to face her, folding my arms. "I did all that shit before. Got into the relationship. Met the family, and they fell in love with me. Only for me to waste ten years of my life in a courtship that went absolutely nowhere besides shacking up together. Ten years I will never get back. I'm through with relationships. Too much of a gamble with my time that I already have little of."

Caira nodded. "I feel you."

"I don't even think I want that life anymore, married with kids." I shrugged. "I'm cool being single, doing my thing, setting my own rules. What Meki and I have is safe, comfortable, and that's what I want. When he or I want it, we get it and that's it. No expectations, no real feelings. Just comfort. And comfort means no drama and I like that. The orgasm without the over commitment. I can just be me around him because I don't care if he likes me for me or not. All I'm concerned about is his big, black, hard di—"

"Dinner's ready," my mother announced as she pushed open the door. "Y'all come on."

"Dang, ma," I said throwing my hands up in the air. "You couldn't have knocked?"

She stepped back and looked up at my door then glanced to her left and right. "Oh I'm sorry... am I in the place where I pay the bills?"

Caira snorted a laugh. I tilted my head to the side and pursed my lips still looking at my mother.

"The two of you come on and eat before the food gets cold."

$$six$$

THE CHIRP of birds outside the window woke me. Before I opened my eyes, I did the usual thing of reaching for my phone only for my grip to meet the air again.

I grunted to myself and slapped my forehead.

"Not again," I muttered, my eyes slowly peeling open.

Fell asleep at his place yet again.

Dammit!

The one thing Caira told me never to do was to spend the night. A booty call was only that... a booty call. It was my responsibility to leave Meki's place before he awoke. Often I succeeded at this, doing our thing and gathering my stuff to leave before the sun rose. But sometimes the sex was that good. The put-you-to-sleep kind of affection that made me sleep well into the breakfast hour.

On the subject of breakfast, I inhaled the air and noticed it smelled different. The lingering aroma of fried eggs and pancakes wafting in the air around his room made me sit up fast.

"What the hell?!"

My eyes moved around Meki's bedroom searching for a shirt to put on and landed on his black tee he wore the day before.

It was the weekend, a few days after Valentine's Day so I didn't hesitate to accept his invitation to chill for the night.

I forced myself to keep busy on V-day to avoid him. I figured if he didn't see me, the chances of us spending the day together were slim.

Valentine's Day was the last day I needed to spend with him. I didn't need him getting any ideas.

But what was with this breakfast, huh? Yes, fine. I should be flattered, right? What woman wouldn't like for a man to prepare a meal for her after laying good pipe the night before?

Well, not me, okay? Not anymore.

I walked out of his bedroom and stepped into his kitchen and found him in front of his stove, shirtless, and only wearing his black cotton boxers.

"Good morning," he said over his shoulder.

"Morning," I said back.

Meki reminded me of a black Ken doll with an edge. Perfectly tatted and sexy in every way. Even the back of him turned me on.

He stood over the fire. Bacon sizzled in an oiled skillet giving the kitchen that good ol' morning aroma.

"Hasn't anyone ever told you never to fry bacon with no clothes on."

He laughed. "It's turkey bacon, less oil and fat. Plus, I never do what people tell me to, anyway."

"Hmph."

He plated the bacon and walked the plates over to the table, placing the plate of bacon down first then the pancakes before returning to his counter for the eggs.

Meki kept his home simple but nice. The only areas in his apartment that looked like a home were his kitchen and bedroom. His bedroom was the most romantic spot in the house. The most romantic bedroom I'd ever seen designed by a man as macho as him. With gray painted walls and bedding to match, the room had a soft look. His velvet area rug below his bed caused no rug burns, I confirmed. And he kept gray candles on his side tables giving the room a genuine touch. Honestly, I believed he put the candles all around for me. He understood how much I loved them. A black dresser and chest completed the design of the room with a simple medium-sized flat screen he kept propped on his chest of drawers.

Out in his living area looked more like an in-home gym. He built a wooden platform in his living room. On that platform, he placed a treadmill and bench press unit with weights stacked beside it.

Dumbbells lined one part of the living area on portable shelves that sat one next to the other.

Back in his kitchen I stared down at the food.

"What's all this?" I asked him once he took his seat at the kitchen table.

"What?" he asked, handing me a plate.

"All of this." I pointed down at the table.

"Breakfast?" he quizzed.

His focus on placing the food on our plates and his nonchalant tone annoyed me.

"Why'd you make it?"

"I was hungry, and I figured if I did my job right last night, you were too."

His arms flexed as he forked the food in his mouth and the sight distracted me a little but not well enough.

"Why do you care?"

He shook his head. "There goes that word again."

"What word?"

"Care."

He looked up in my eyes and dropped his fork. The sound of the silverware clattering against the rim of his plate echoed around the kitchen as he gave me his full attention.

"Well," I said, arching my brows, "why do you? You didn't have to do all this."

"All what, Cadence? Make food? What's the big deal?"

I looked away. "I don't know. It seems like..."

"Like what?"

I looked at him. "Like you're catching feelings."

Meki sat back in his seat and stared at me for a moment, pushing the tip of his tongue against the inside of his cheek.

"The way you looked at me at the park the other day we went running," I continued, "what was that?"

"So, I'm supposed to feel absolutely nothing for you."

"No... I mean yes, you're supposed to feel nothing... at all."

"And you feel nothing for me?"

"Nothing."

"Oh really?" He shook his head. "You allow me to have my way with you almost every night," he said leaning forward.

I looked away again.

"I'm more familiar with your body than probably you are. Sex is sex, yes, I get it. But it's a feeling, nonetheless. How can you truly enjoy me if you feel nothing? How is it I can make you feel everything when I'm inside of you but you can sit across from me with a straight face and say you feel nothing for me? I can't even force myself to understand that."

When I hadn't focused back on him he said, "Cadence, woman... you better look at me when I'm talking to you. For real."

"Or what," I said, turning my head to face him.

He smirked and ran his palm down his face slow. "Do I have feelings for you? Maybe a little. I am human. I've known you for a while now and I've seen you in ways that others haven't. So yes, I may have some kind of feelings for you and I'm sure you do too. But your ego is too big to admit that."

"Ego?" I countered. "You're telling me about ego? Your ego is bigger than this whole block.

"And you love it."

"Debatable."

"Admit you're falling for me."

"Ha! I'd rather die first."

"Don't say that." He glared at me from across the table. "Never say that again around me."

I stared at him for a moment then scoffed. "It was a joke. Calm down, geez."

"Why must this always be the thing we do? If we aren't fucking, we're bickering. Going back and forth over stupid shit that's not even important. You love to argue. Can't we eat in peace?"

"I didn't ask you to make this for me, Meki. Why does my attitude matter, anyway? It should have no effect on your meal."

Meki shook his head then turned his attention on his plate. He stabbed his fork into his bacon and eggs and forked his breakfast into his mouth. He couldn't mask his anger if he tried as he chewed his food harder than usual.

"You know what, I'll leave." I pushed my chair back and stood up. As I walked past him he caught me by the arm and pulled me down onto his lap.

"Meki—"

"Stay and eat with me... please."

"No, I have to—"

"Please," he stressed.

"I thought you didn't beg."

He sighed then pressed his forehead to my back. "A man can make an exception, can't he?"

I took a deep breath and glanced at him over my shoulder. He smiled at me and I did my best to fight the smile pulling at my lips but it was no use.

"Fine," I said low. "You made the food. So, I guess I could just eat it so it doesn't go to waste."

He pressed his mouth to the back of my shoulder and left a kiss.

"I appreciate it," he said.

Meki leaned forward, pulled my plate in front of me, and returned to eating his food while I sat on his lap.

I might not have admitted I had feelings for him in that moment. But I could admit that being there with his arm around me felt right.

A little too right.

seven

IT HAD BEEN a month since that moment in Meki's kitchen. After all the back and forth, we ended the morning by hooking up once we cleaned our plates... right there on the kitchen table. On top of the table, hunched over it, him sitting on the chair in front of it and me straddling him and riding until my hips ached.

I got mine every which way and then some.

No matter how much I enjoyed him, when we finished, and I was back in my place alone, his words played in my mind on repeat like a scratched record. What he said to me I couldn't shake. He admitted, without actually admitting, he was catching feelings for me.

Shit.

Now a Thursday, as I sat at my desk, my work completed, leaving the second half of the day free for me to indulge in 90s reruns on Hulu, I wrestled with thoughts of him.

This wasn't the first time my mind wandered to Meki, and I tried my hardest not to think of him. One time I made the mistake of giving into those thoughts, calling him and him suggesting we grab lunch together. Never made that error again.

What was I thinking?

"Cadence," my supervisor Lana said at my door.

Busy daydreaming, I didn't notice her standing there.

"Um... Cadence?" Lana snapped her fingers, and I pulled myself back to reality.

I lifted my hand to my face and pinched the space between my eyes.

She snickered. "Everything okay?"

"Yeah," I said. "Sorry about that. I might need a little more coffee."

"I could use a cup too," she said, tossing her blond hair over her shoulder and smiling at me. "How about you grab two fresh brews and meet me in my office? I need to speak with you about something."

I swallowed hard. "Uh... yeah... sure."

Meet her in her office? For what?

There were only two reasons I needed to join Lana in her office and that was to discuss firing someone or for a meeting about a new client. But I usually received an email before those sit downs.

Am I getting fired?

I'd survived the biggest layoff wave in the company's history the year before after the Christmas holiday where we'd gotten rid of fifteen engineers, three managers, and two coordinators.

Was there another wave coming? I wasn't ready.

I filled two company mugs with coffee in the break room and walked them over to Lana's office. My knees wobbled the entire way as I struggled to balance my nervous self on the heels of my Jimmy Choo pumps.

"Perfect," she said as she stood up from her desk, her hand extended for her mug.

"A splash of milk, a drop of cream, and two sugars right?" I asked, handing it to her.

She smiled, pleased.

I was about to suck-up the best way I knew how. Do you understand how expensive New York is? How hard it is to maintain a job in this city? And with my retail addiction? Yeah, I'd humble myself enough to kiss her ass to keep my direct deposit intact.

"That's exactly how I like my coffee made, thank you." She blushed. "Have a seat."

"Okay."

She took a sip of her coffee and so did I.

"Cadence, I'm very pleased with your role here but I feel you aren't being challenged enough as a coordinator manager."

"Challenged? I'm challenged."

"Someone of your skill set deserves something better. A place they can be at their best and in a way that complements the company they are with."

Shit, she is firing me.

"That's why I've decided to—"

"Please don't fire me," I blurted.

She tilted her head to the right and stared at me.

"If it's longer hours you need, then I can give it. Shorter vacations, no problem."

Did I just say that?

In that moment, Meki's taunts of me working like a slave, running to the plantation on days I set aside to rest, stalked my thoughts. I always took his words as light-hearted play but in that moment I was sure enough feeling that way.

"Fire you?" she echoed. Soon she burst into laughter then balanced her upper body on her elbows and leaned on her desk in my direction. "Cadence, I want to promote you dear."

My jaw dropped. "Really?"

"Yes," she said through her giggles. "Why on earth would you convince yourself that I'd want to fire you?"

"Well, you said I wasn't being challenged, and you wanted me to complement the company I was with."

"Yes, this company. Just in a bigger role."

I smiled.

"I'm aware of your afternoon TV times you've been enjoying during business hours."

I cringed, closing my eyes and gritting my teeth.

She laughed. "It's okay. I do it too occasionally."

"Sorry."

"Really it's fine. But I think the extra time you have could be used for better and to your benefit. I want to offer you the role of our west coast Resource Director—"

"Oh my God, what?!"

She nodded.

"Yes, I'll take it—"

"There is one catch."

"I don't even care what it is... but what is it?"

Lana laughed.

"Longer hours? More meetings?"

"The position requires you to work from our office in San Francisco."

I stopped breathing for only a moment. All I could do was blink repeatedly in response.

"San Francisco..." I finally said, "as in California?"

"Yes, California. As we detailed in the company memo, we opened our new office over there at the start of this year. Seems San Francisco is booming with business. Many of our New York clients are relocating their headquarters there so we want to stay ahead of the competition and set solid roots out in the west too. We have one of our managers from the Arizona office who has been traveling back and forth to manage both offices but now we need someone more permanent and you'd be perfect for the role."

"Wow," I said sitting back in my seat. "California."

She nodded slow.

"As in 3,000 miles away from New York... California."

Lana let a little laugh vibrate in her throat.

"It's a big deal." She interlocked her fingers in front of her. "I'll give you time to mull it over but I will need your decision before the end of May no later than June. I believe that's ample time for you to decide if California is a good move for you."

"Yeah, definitely a good amount of time to come to a decision. Thank you so much for considering me for this Lana. I really appreciate it."

"Just keep up the great work, Cadence. You've earned this. So, really you should thank yourself."

I smiled and stood up from my seat.

She pointed at my mug on her desk and said, "Don't forget your coffee. Can't have you in a daze before you clock out."

I forced out a laugh as I grabbed my cup.

Meki.

On my way out of her office and headed back to mine his name and his face was the first thing plaguing my mind.

Not my parents. Not even Caira.

Meki.

That one person and how they would take this news kept popping up in my head. And I couldn't understand why his opinion or even his approval mattered when I didn't care what and how he felt about this.

Or did I?

Meki.

I'm not sure if I could leave him.

Did I just think that?

eight

APRIL 14TH. Ever since I learned the significance of that date I couldn't forget it even if I tried. I'd been counting down the days until the 14th, unintentionally, and finally the date had arrived. The night at least.

Meki's birthday. His 32nd born day, and he chose to spend the night with me. Earlier that day, friends and his brothers took him out to brunch. You know, rich people's stuff. With these guys, the option was an insanely expensive night on the town or a simple get-together like a brunch. Meki would skip it all together but he did enjoy their tamed meet-ups because deep down he knew he loved being around them.

For the night, we stayed in. My place and in my bedroom. I asked him what he wanted for his birthday and he said being with me would do. So we planned to chill for the night watching something on Netflix via my Amazon Fire TV Stick.

I suggested we pick a horror flick.

No, viewing gore at night wasn't normally my thing, but I needed to occupy our time with something less romantic so the sex would be wild... like I preferred our hookups to be.

We spread out a blanket over my bed covers and placed a bunch of snacks on top. On any other day, Meki ate clean. Brown rice, baked fish or chicken. No pork or red meat, hardly any dairy. You know, the usual health nut bit. Sometimes, he'd go weeks eating no flesh at all. He was better than me.

I looked over at him as he tossed a buttered popcorn into his mouth. I snickered then reached for the Oreos, peeling open the package of chocolate sandwich cookies.

"This is dope," he said. "I think it's cute you remembered my birthday."

I shrugged. "It's an easy day to recall."

"Not really."

I rolled my eyes, picking up the Fire TV Stick remote and clicking through the movie titles. "I was thinking we could press play on SAW."

He looked over at me with knitted brows and shook his head. "Nah."

He grabbed the Fire stick remote out of my hand then padded the buttons with his thumb until the highlight landed on *Love Jones.*

"Let's watch this instead."

I turned my head slow to my right to look at him.

"It's my birthday," he said before tossing another popcorn into his mouth and chewing with a smile.

I sighed. "Fine. Whatever."

"Fine. Whatever." He mocked in a forced high pitch tone.

I shoved him and he laughed.

We were never great at watching movies together. Meki and I were the epitome of Netflix and chill. We'd always start off completely into a film, watching the movie until the movie ended up watching us. Thirty minutes into *Love Jones,* right around the time Nia Long and Larenz Tate hooked up for the first time after their first date, Meki buried his fingers in my hair, his lips on my neck.

I moaned my delight into the space around us and he groaned in response.

"Why is this the only time I can soften you up?" he asked in my ear before leaving a kiss there.

I bit my lip in response to the warmth of his mouth near my lobe. He knew that was my spot.

"I don't want to fight with you anymore," he whispered.

"Liar. You like the make up sex too much to want to skip the fight before the fuck."

He let a sexy laugh vibrate in his throat as his hand cupped my breast.

"Mmm." I moaned, closing my eyes and giving into him.

That hand of his slid from my breast, over my navel, and down to between my thighs. The lights were off so the back-light from the TV lit up the room. I burned a candle for the night and my eyes focused on the tiny flickering flame moving with the room's air.

Meki teased me, playing with my clit against the fabric of my varsity shorts and panties. He made it clear he had plans to make me beg for it.

"Do you want me?"

"You know the answer to that," I exhaled.

"But..." Meki licked me from my collarbone to the space just below my ear and my walls pulsed in response. "I want to hear you say it."

I sighed.

"It's my birthday."

"Are you going to use that line the whole night?"

"Mm-hmm."

I giggled then closed my eyes again. "I want you."

"How bad?"

"Real bad."

Meki kissed my chin then brought his mouth to mine. He pecked me twice. Soft kisses that almost made me squirt in my panties.

On my lips he said, "Tell me your pussy is mine."

I opened my eyes to his, our focus locked on each other.

"You want me to lie to you?" I asked.

He smirked. "I want you to say what's true." He bit his bottom lip and tightened his grip between my thighs. "Tell me it's mine."

Silence.

He chuckled softly. "Come on, play nice. It's my—"

"Birthday?" I finished

He winked, and I rolled my eyes.

"Fine," I whispered. "It's yours."

He pushed his hand behind the band of my varsity shorts and into my panties. I was wet, dripping for him and he groaned on my neck after his fingers became slick with my honey.

"Good girl."

By the time the movie credits rolled, I was on my side with Meki deep inside of me, singer Lauryn Hill's voice whispering through my TV's speakers as she belted out the lyrics to her song, "The Sweetest Thing."

So appropriate.

He laid behind me, moving in and out with my hip tight in his grip.

Meki moved his hand to my face to hold my jaw as he served me more of him from the back. He used my jaw to turn my face to face his, so he could kiss me.

He penetrated me both orally and physically, mimicking his strokes with that thick wet muscle in his mouth.

Meki worked me over like it was my birthday instead of his. He growled each time my walls contracted around his shaft. He tightened his grip around my jaw when I'd gasp at how deep he gave himself to me.

"Who do you belong to, Cae?" he asked me in my ear.

I could barely get my thoughts in order with him stroking me to a surging orgasm. This one hit me different from the others. The waves of pleasure took time to build and with each delayed moment, the feeling got more intense. I curled my toes and grabbed the bed sheets between my fingers to brace myself.

"Tell me Cadence."

"You," I whispered. "I belong to you."

He growled then went deeper. "I love how you feel."

"Ooohh, I love you too..."

I gasped the moment the words left my lips. If those four words had strings attached to them, I'd pull them back in my mouth and down my throat.

It was like the world stood still and time froze.

Meki stopped mid-stroke and paused in place. I turned, and he looked down at me. We held our stares making the seconds feel more like hours.

He pulled out of me slow.

I immediately turned on my back and propped myself up by the elbows, my eyes still on his.

All I heard in my room was the song "I Got a Love Jones For You" playing as the last of the credits scrolled up my flat screen. That, and the sound of the two of us breathing hard.

"Umm..." I tried to find the words, but they were all jumbled up in my thoughts. The one thing I kept hearing was my voice professing my love for someone I didn't even like.

He sat there for a moment, his brows set in confusion.

"I didn't mean that—"

"Shh," he shushed, looking me in my eyes. I stopped speaking when he pressed his finger to my lips. Meki slid his hand from my mouth to the side of my cheeks right before he leaned forward and crushed his lips against mine. He encouraged me to recline flat on the bed by leaning the weight of his body against me. Meki had one hand on my cheek and the other mapping the spine of my back until he made me arch it high. He positioned himself on top of me and slid into me slow, gentler than he'd ever done before. I welcomed every inch of him, my walls pulsed as they accommodated his length.

He delivered long deep thrusts. Elemental, his movements set off electric charges throughout my body. In my mind, we were no longer just there on my bed. We were out in another world, our world, communicating physically and innately. The shit was sensual. Rubbing my thighs as he sped up the pace. He slipped out of me only for a second, so he could savor me with his tongue. I never thought sex could get better with him until I experienced the flick of his tongue moments after having him inside of me. He took his time down there, licking between my lips slow and lapping me up like I was his favorite movie snack. He toyed with my clit with the tip of his tongue and moaned when my nub swelled from sensitivity on his taste buds.

"I'm coming," I announced and he let me, right on his lips.

Seconds later he interlocked his fingers with mine as he tunneled into me and continued to break me down with each passing minute. He moved slow, keeping his eyes on me until I couldn't take the sight of him deep stroking me so good with so much desire in his eyes. By the time I succumbed to the crashing wave of my climax drowning me in satisfaction, I'd forgotten all about what I'd said to him. And I hoped he did too.

nine

A FEW DAYS LATER, a Tuesday night, I laid in bed alone. I did well to avoid Meki after his birthday night. No matter how hard I tried, I couldn't stop replaying the words I said to him. More than that, I found it impossible to forget the way he felt that night. He sexed me better than ever before.

Sex with him was always great. But the night of his birthday he raised the bar previously set by him. And the aftershocks... they wouldn't stop. Every time I thought about the man I was transported back to that night. The memory so vivid, I shivered from thoughts of him.

Tuesday night, I unlocked my iPhone and tapped into my Instagram app. I'd been so busy those past few months I unintentionally neglected my account. Anyone who needed to contact me had my phone number. So I didn't feel like I missed much.

While scrolling through my feed, mindlessly liking pics, I came across a photo of my ex-boyfriend, Terrell.

I hadn't spoken to Terrell since that day I left him holding his forehead after I tossed our apartment keys at his face. I found myself occasionally reminiscing about him after our breakup. Even after learning he'd moved on with some random woman soon after we parted. It was whatever. Couldn't blame him. It's not like I've been celibate since we ended things.

In this recent photo he stood in the weights room at a gym. His face wasn't in the shot but he did capture his body. Terrell always prided himself on his workout routine. He visited the inside of his neighborhood gym every day except for Sundays. Terrell took that day off to rest.

It had been a year since we'd seen each other and the year had been good to him. Based on the photo, his abs were tighter his arms even more fit than when I last saw him. And there wasn't a filter in the world creative enough to fake that.

I hesitated to tap the heart beneath his picture, but gave in to the sight of him and double tapped his photo, anyway. Not even five minutes later my phone dinged with a direct message from him.

My heart felt like it dropped several floors below me. I clicked the home button on my iPhone and threw my phone to my bed.

"Shit," I said to myself.

My phone dinged again, and then a third time with two more messages.

I took a deep breath, picked it up, tapped back into the app and then clicked into my DMs.

Terrell: What's good Cadence?

Me: Hey

Terrell: It's been a while. What's new?

Oh nothing. I've been carrying on a complicated relationship with my next-door neighbor and I accidentally told him I loved him while coming. You know, the usual.

Me: Nothing much. Just grinding and climbing that corpo-rate ladder.

He was quiet for a moment, no disappearing, reappearing "typing" text to hint that he was in the process of typing something.

Finally he responded.

Terrell: I miss you.

I furrowed my brows and stared at those three words.

Terrell and my relationship was good for what it was. There wasn't a single time I wanted out of our union other than when I finally realized how much time I wasted on him. He refused to give me what I desired back then, stability.

Now, I'd morphed into a different Cadence. A Cadence he probably wouldn't even recognize.

I missed him too, a little. I wouldn't tell him that. Not word for word at least. But curiosity left me wondering just what kind of interaction we would have when we both wanted the same thing, no commitment.

Me: Same.

Terrell: *male cartwheel emoji*

Me: *laughing emoji*

Terrell: We should link up. What are you doing this weekend?

On any other weekend, I'd either be hanging out with Caira or Meki. In that moment, I had no solid plans.

Me: Nothing right now

Terrell: Let's meet up for coffee at our usual place on Saturday at 6 p.m.

I accepted Terrell's invitation. We set a time and made arrangements to hang out that weekend.

* * *

"You look good Cadence," Terrell told me as we sat across from each other at Breukelen, a black-owned coffee shop in the Crown Heights section of Brooklyn. We went there often when we dated, having lived in the area. It had been a year, but my old stomping grounds changed drastically in that short time.

A lot more hippies and police presence watered down what was once one of the most culturally rich areas to chill. That was okay, at least Breukelen remained the same.

Terrell and I arrived at the coffee shop after breakfast hour, but I refused to pass up the opportunity to indulge in the shop's popular breakfast in a cup. Terrell and I always went on coffee dates. Every weekend, we'd grab mugs of coffee at the coffee shop. The barista would artfully design cute maple leaves on the surface of our coffees using creamer. For food, they'd fry up eggs and veggies, with bacon for the meat eaters, and put all that goodness in a paper cup for the customer's consumption.

Visiting the café offered a dope experience and added to the culture of Crown Heights.

"You look good too." I blushed at his compliment. "I see you've been keeping up with your workout regimen."

Terrell lifted his arm and flexed his bicep.

I snickered.

His arms were buff and ripped with muscles. They were sexy. Not as sexy as Meki's but definitely a beautiful sight.

"So, what's new with you... other than work?" he asked, taking a sip of his coffee.

"Nothing much."

"Seeing anybody?"

"Yeah," I said looking away. "But nothing serious."

"Yeah, I know how that goes. I'm surprised you're still single. Thought you would have clubbed someone over the head and forced them into marriage by now." He laughed.

I stared at him forcing myself to share in the humor of his words but finding it impossible to laugh too.

"Funny." I rolled my eyes. "No, I'm not really interested in that anymore. Proved to be a complete waste of time."

"Hmph." He shrugged. "I really didn't want for us to break up because of that, Cadence. Would have loved to see how far we could've gotten in our relationship."

"How far we could've gotten?" I repeated. "Really? Well, I thought marriage was the destination, but... whatever."

"But since you don't want that anymore, there's no reason to talk about it right?"

I forced a smile then looked away.

What am I doing here?

A couple sitting in one corner of the café, drinking coffee with their fingers interlocked caught my eye. The guy looked at his woman like she was the only person in the coffee shop. It was sweet.

"So what are you into these days?" Terrell asked, pulling my attention back on him.

I shrugged. "Just chillin'."

"You want company after this?"

He winked at me and my walls pulsed. Not as hard as they would have pulsed if Meki had said something similar, but it was a reaction.

Why do I keep comparing them?

That question alone made me curious about how opened I was with the new lifestyle I swore I was all about living. You know, sexually liberated, not committed to one person, blah, blah, blah.

Meki and I weren't in a relationship. I'd fucked up by saying those three words to him but I didn't really mean them, right?

Right.

Right?

"Cadence?" Terrell quizzed, placing his hand on top of mine. "Did you hear me?"

"Yeah, sorry about that."

"Where'd you go just now?"

I turned my hand to offer him my palm, and he took my hand. "Just lost in my thoughts of you and what having your company might be like tonight."

His smile stretched from cheek-to-cheek and I returned one back.

"Let's get out of here. Your place or mine?"

I bit the side of my bottom lip thinking. This was a power play. There was no way I'd go back to our old apartment. Just standing at the threshold would bring back a flood of memories, bad ones, and all reminding me of the day I left for good. Besides, it was a Saturday evening. I knew for sure Meki would be at the gym. He always was at that hour.

The decision seemed like a clear one, so I believed.

"Mine," I replied.

ten

"THIS IS a nice block and your building is kinda dope. You doing all right," Terrell said as we climbed the last flight of stairs in my apartment building.

"Yeah," I said, fishing through my leather purse for my keys. "When I first moved here, there were only a few people living in the building. There still aren't many tenants but, it's a good spot."

We arrived in front of my apartment door and I still couldn't locate my keys. I glanced over my shoulder at Terrell who stood there, grinning at me. He moved in close shortly after that and wrapped his arms around my waist, bringing his lips to my neck to kiss.

I giggled and my voice echoed around us. "Come on, stop that."

Suddenly I heard the click of locks behind us.

Meki's door.

Fuck!

I held onto my inhale a little longer as the door opened and Meki stood at his threshold behind Terrell and me. Fully dressed in workout gear, the strap of Meki's gym bag laid across his chest.

His eyes bounced between Terrell and mine then landed back on me. He didn't say a word for five seconds which seemed more like five hours.

He settled his eyes on Terrell and looked Terrell up and down. Terrell squared his chest and did the same.

Seeing the two men I'd been with intimately and in front of me was so surreal. My past and my present right there in the flesh.

"And who the hell are you?" Meki asked Terrell.

"Excuse me?" Terrell replied.

"Oh my bad." Meki clapped his hands once and took a deep breath in response. "I'm addressing the wrong person."

Meki glared at me with a tight jaw and said, "Who the hell is this?"

"Do you two *know* each other like that?" Terrell turned to face me.

I avoided eye contact with him and instead chose to focus on Meki.

"I thought you were at the gym."

"I was waiting for you. I haven't seen or spoken to you since—"

Terrell cleared his throat, his way of reminding us he was still there.

"Terrell," I said pointing at Meki, "this is Meki. Meki, Terrell."

Meki's eyes widened. "Your ex-boyfriend Terrell?!"

Terrell folded his arms and focused on me. "So y'all do know each other like that. Well enough for him to know who I am."

"This is so weird," I mumbled while pinching the bridge of my nose. "Terrell, let's just go inside."

"Terrell let's just go inside?" Meki echoed. "What the fuck are you doing, Cadence?"

When I said nothing he brought his hand to his mouth to cup. "I can't believe this shit. You just told me that you love—"

Meki stopped himself from continuing by clenching his jaw and shaking his head.

"You know what... whatever. Have fun," Meki said, turning briefly to lock his door.

Terrell's eyes moved between Meki and me.

I wanted to say something, anything but I couldn't find the words to speak. Meki took one last look at me before shaking his head again then jogging down the case of stairs toward the lobby.

Terrell pointed in the direction Meki went and I turned to face my door, my eyes down in my bag as I continued searching for my keys.

* * *

Inside my apartment, Terrell's eyes were everywhere. He walked into my living room, his attention focused on the decor pieces and the way I arranged my furniture around the room.

"I gotta admit," he said, shrugging off his leather jacket and tossing it on the couch. "That's the one thing I miss about staying with you, your designing skills. You always kept the place nice, clean, and looking right."

I screwed my face up at his comment. He made it seem like I was his former maid or something.

"I never had to pick things up after myself because you always did it for me. You were a good girlfriend, man. For real."

He walked up and pulled me close, pecking me on the lips. I tried to lose myself in his touch but everything about the situation rubbed me wrong. Terrell's words, the look on Meki's face. Standing there with Terrell's mouth on me, I second guessed my decision to meet up with him much less bring him to my place.

Terrell kissed my neck when I asked, "Do you miss me because you miss my company or do you miss the things I did for you?"

"A little of both," he said between his kisses.

I exhaled sharply, disappointed.

"My place, your old home, is missing that woman's touch. And since you don't care that much about marriage anymore..."

He paused speaking to back me against my living room wall to run his hands up my torso toward my breasts. "We can pick right up where we left off at and do that happily ever after thing. Only our version. Feel me?"

I gritted my teeth and pressed my hands to his chest pushing him off me. "No, Terrell. I don't feel you. And tonight, you won't be feeling me either, sweetheart."

"Huh? What?"

"How could I be so stupid?"

He stood there staring at me. His hard-on tenting his jeans, brows set in confusion. "What you mean?"

"What I mean is this was a mistake. Talking to you again, agreeing to meet up with you, having you here. All a mistake."

I took large steps toward my couch where he dropped his leather jacket, grabbed it, and walked it over to him, holding it out for him to take. "You have to go. I was not thinking straight when I agreed to see you again."

He snatched his jacket from me. "You fucked that guy across the hall, didn't you?"

"Now *that* is none of your concern, is it?"

"Yeah you did. Damn! So, you can give him ass and expect nothing in return, but for me, I gotta put a ring on it?"

I laughed. "Wow. You know what the difference is between you and Meki? He expects nothing else from me. You though," I said poking him on his chest, "you want for me to prepare a meal, pick up after you, and wash your dirty fucking underwear after you give me your weak ass orgasms."

"Hey! Shit, at least I gave you multiples, aight?" He shrugged. "And what's the problem with wanting all that stuff, anyway?"

"The problem is you want wife shit without offering concrete commitment, something to build on, and I'm not about to fall into that trap again."

I turned him by his shoulders and pushed him toward my door. "It was nice seeing you again Terrell, kind of, but you gotta go, bruh."

"Aight, aight, hold up," he said turning to face me. "Before I go, I gotta ask you something really important." Terrell took my hand and brought me close. "I don't know if I'll ever see you again so..." He gave me a longing gaze and brought his hand to my cheek to caress.

Terrell asked, "What's the name of that detergent you used to use on my clothes?"

My jaw dropped.

"I can't remember the brand but I used to love how my clothes smelled after you washed them with the detergent and I can't seem to find it anywhere. Was it like a special version of Tide?"

"Are you serious?"

"Yeah. Help a brother out Cadence! Women loved how good I smelled when they sat next to me on the train after you washed my clothes with that stuff."

"Get out!" I yelled.

He shook his head and stepped outside turning to face me. "On some real shit, you're trippin' right now. But you have my info. Call me when you're out of your feelings or whatever. I'm still down to rekindle if you are, feel me?"

I closed the door in his face and turned to press my back to my door sliding down it until I plopped to the floor beneath me.

I slapped myself on the forehead twice.

"What did I just do?"

eleven

TWO SATURDAYS LATER, I sat across from Caira at dinner. We chose a simple Thai restaurant to chill at for the evening. Caira and I had nothing else going on that day and sitting in the house eating takeout when the weather finally matched spring was a no-go. So we hopped in an Uber and settled on heading cross town to the Drunken Noodle, a tiny Asian spot on Flatbush Avenue.

"So what's going on with you?" I asked her before taking a sip of my Thai iced tea. "Anything interesting happen this week?"

"Yup," she said, before biting into her spring roll. "I found out I'm pregnant."

I coughed incessantly. The sip I took went down the wrong pipe the moment I gasped while swallowing. My shock had more to do with how lax she announced her pregnancy than with what she actually said.

"Are you okay?" she asked pushing her chair back.

I lifted a finger, signaling for her to stay seated. The rim of my glass was to my mouth as I sipped just enough water to clear my airway.

"Pregnant?" was the first thing I said when I gained my composure. "Did I hear that right?"

Caira laughed. "See this is the reason I hesitated with telling you. I knew you wouldn't take it well."

"Pregnant?" I repeated.

"Yes, Cadence. Pregnant." She shrugged then looked out into the distance. "About ten weeks."

My eyes bulged out, and she laughed some more.

"Caira... girl, stop playing with me. You're not serious."

She dipped her hand into her purse and pulled out a sonogram placing it down on the table in front of me. "Meet the new addition to our family."

"You're keeping it?"

She frowned. "Cadence don't ask me that shit. Of course I'm keeping it."

I covered my forehead with my hand and shook my head. "I have so many questions."

"Naturally."

Our waitress returned to our table with our bowls of Pad Thai. Caira left me so much in shock I couldn't even muster up a thank you or to even pick up my fork to eat.

"Who's the father?" I asked.

"You've never met him. Some guy I exchanged numbers with after meeting at a mall three months ago."

I slacked my jaw then shook my head. "Caira."

"Hold up now bitch, don't judge me." She pointed.

"I'm not judging," I said throwing my hands up in supplication. "Promise. This is just... crazy. You can at least admit that this is crazy, right?"

"It is. That I can agree with you on." She laughed.

"You know Auntie V is gonna kill you, right?" I said, referring to her mother, Vivian.

She shrugged. "I'm 34, Cadence. I'm a grown ass woman. Plus she's been pestering me with questions about when I'm gonna meet a man and give her some grandbabies."

"Knowing Auntie V, I think she was expecting you to complete one little step before giving her those grandbabies Cai."

"Fuck the steps. Fuck the rules."

I stared at her.

"When have you ever known me to do anything in order?"

I bit the inside of my cheek. "Never."

"Exactly."

"But this is a baby. A whole human. A new responsibility."

She nodded, smiling.

"Are you ready for all that?"

"I am. I'm getting older cuzzo. Life gotta switch up a little. This might be just what I need to slow down and change perspective, you know?"

"Hmph. Crazy as it sounds, I feel you."

A few minutes into our meal we talked about the baby and the thrilled father who couldn't wait to be a daddy. After a lengthy discussion about what pushing a baby out would do to her vagina, which she insisted snaps back, our conversation switched to Meki.

I'd told her all about my decision to go out with Terrell. She scolded me. But her scold of me was nothing compared to the mental assault I inflicted on myself after Terrell left my apartment.

"Spoke to Meki yet?"

I shook my head.

"You sure fucked that up royally."

I looked up at her then rolled my eyes.

"I gotta keep it real with you, Cadence. You had a good thing going with Meki. But you had to prove something to yourself that didn't need proving."

"Wasn't it you who told me not to get caught up with him?"

"But you did. At that point, you should've just went with the flow. It worked for you two."

"I told you, I didn't want a relationship. Meki was flexing like he did. I'll give him a few more days. I'm sure eventually he'll come around. He's just pissed right now."

"I'm not sure, Cadence. Men are weird like that. They can fuck a whole fleet of women but expect each one to not even entertain conversations with the next dude."

"That's stupid," I said sipping my drink.

The buzz of restaurant chatter around us grew in volume so I pushed my chair closer to the table so Caira could continue to hear my words.

"What do they expect for us to do while they're out there fucking the next girl?" I asked. "Sit home and wait for our turn?"

Caira pursed her lips. "Men. But he wasn't seeing anybody else, Cadence. Only you. He obviously saw something more there."

"Yeah..." I said low. "I know."

I looked down at my hands, my eyes watering. "I'm gonna get him to answer his door tonight when I get back home... so we can talk."

* * *

As planned, after returning home I stopped in front of Meki's door, knocking on it a few times. Unplanned, he didn't answer.

Oh, he was in there.

I heard footsteps as he approached the door to peek through the peephole. And when he saw it was me, he mumbled something to himself on the other side of his closed door before walking away. I left well enough alone.

Around midnight, after fighting back the urge to knock on his door a second time, with enough convincing, I climbed into bed and decided I would try him again in the morning.

A few hours later, the squeak of bedsprings and the backside of a headboard woke me from sleep. The headboard banged against the wall behind my bed. The banging started out as light thuds but as the bedspring's squeaks continued, the headboard banging got progressively louder. I sat up in bed, sleep still in my eyes. It was three in the morning, still dark outside.

"No he didn't," I said to myself. "No he fucking did not bring a girl home!"

Moans accompanied the sound of the headboard assaulting my wall soon after.

"Oooh, Meki, right there. Right. There!" a female yelled on the other side of my wall.

Meki's bedroom was behind that wall.

I felt like I'd been placed into one of those machines that crushed cars. Those sex noises coming from Meki's apartment knocked the air out of me. The rhythm of my heart sped up as her moaning got louder, the headboard hammering the wall not missing a beat.

"Oh baby," she yelled. "You feel so good."

"You like that, huh?" he panted.

The moment I heard his voice my eyes pooled with tears and all it took was one blink for the tears to slide down my face.

"How about this?" he asked in between his moans. "You like this too?"

"Yes, yes... Oooh yessss!"

I pressed my hand to my chest as if it would stop the pain in my heart. It was like being in a wet dream hearing him sex someone else. Her wet dream and my nightmare, actually.

She screamed his name, and he growled from the pleasure sexing her provided.

The two of them went at it for a few more minutes until silence settled over my room again.

I pushed myself up then stood on my mattress to press my ear to the wall behind my bed. Muffled smacking noises sounded on the other side of my wall. That and soft moans. They were talking to each other but the thickness of the wall separating our rooms made it difficult to make out what they were saying to one another.

Just the thought of him being intimate with someone else broke me a little. I tried not to care, but it was impossible. My skin grew hot, my heart was beating so hard I could feel it in my ears. I wanted to tear everything in my room that wasn't nailed to something to shreds.

The longer I sat there, the air in my room seemed to get less and less. So, I snatched up my blanket and pillow, and stomped my way into my living room, deciding to spend the rest of the night out on my couch crying into the cushions.

The next morning, I checked the time of the first yoga class at the YogaWorks studio closest to my neighborhood. I usually frequented the one in Brooklyn Heights.

My mind was boggled with the shit I witnessed the night before, my heart heavy. I didn't get a wink of sleep. Curiosity about Meki and his lady friend preoccupied my thoughts.

What they were doing? If they were still in his place having sex several hours later?

When I couldn't shake the menacing thoughts, I left the apartment to clear my mind with hopes a downward dog and proud warrior would help.

Fully dressed, I pulled opened the door to find Meki and his lady friend standing at the threshold in front of his apartment. I saw her back first. But when she turned around, I recognized her instantly.

"Hi! Cadence, correct?" Giselle quizzed.

How could I forget her?

Long dark hair, slim and tall. She styled herself in jeans and a black tee which she wore beneath a denim jacket. Riding boots completed her getup. I guess she believed she came suited up for her trip to the hood to be among the paupers. Her words.

"I had no idea you lived right next door to Meki," she said, grinning.

"I bet," I mumbled.

"I hope we weren't too loud last night," she said with a giggle.

Giselle had a snide grin on her lips like she'd won a game show. It took everything in me not to lunge at her and to clean the hallway floor with her face.

I looked up at Meki instead and he stared right at me.

I shook my head.

"Anyway, hon," she said turning to face Meki. "Call me tonight. Let's set up a time to meet for dinner. In Long Island though, okay?"

Meki nodded, still looking at me.

I couldn't stop my eyes from tearing up and he noticed, his hard stare softening.

Giselle balanced herself a little on the arches of her feet so she could peck him on his lips. He let her but didn't kiss her back.

"It was nice running into you again, Cadence," she said.

As she pranced down the staircase with some extra pep in her step she added, "It's amazing what a few months can change, huh girl? Just like I said. I love it when I'm right."

I rolled my eyes and folded my arms.

"Good seeing you Cadence," she said before moving out of sight.

"I knocked on your door last night," I said to him once we were alone.

He leaned against the panel of his door and buried his hands in the pockets of his gray sweatpants. "As you can see I've been busy."

I curled the right side of my lip up, turning to face my door, shutting and locking it. Really, I was trying to wipe the tears that were threatening to fall from my eyes without him seeing.

Why the hell was I crying?

"So that's what you want, huh?" I turned to face him, fixing the strap of my yoga mat holder. "Her?"

"You're not the only one who can call up friends at the last minute to chill," he said with finger quotes.

I shook my head.

"Isn't this what you wanted? Me not catching feelings and shit? So here, proof I'm not. It's all good, Cadence, right?"

"No, because Terrell didn't fuck me!" I yelled.

I cleared my throat as my voice echoed around me. That was embarrassing.

"If you care to know, I sent him home," I said low. "Before anything happened between him and me, I sent him home."

Meki broke eye contact with me, his jaw slacked a little. His eyes moved erratically along the floor beneath us when he asked, "You did? Look, I thought—"

"Whatever."

"Cadence..."

His voice trailed off behind me as I brushed past him and ran down the stairs, jumping over two steps at a time.

I refused to stick around long enough to hear what else he had to say after that.

He didn't owe me any explanations. It's like he said, *this* was what I wanted. I just didn't know what *this* was anymore.

twelve

A FEW DAYS LATER, I heard a knock at my apartment's door. It was around 8 p.m., so I already knew who it was.

Meki.

Meki and I had done an excellent job of avoiding one another. Never knowing when we were coming or going. I wasn't sure about him, but I would tiptoe around my apartment in hopes he wouldn't notice when I was there.

I put in longer hours at work that week adding to my absence at home. But despite all I did to keep my schedule full, my heart still felt empty.

Not seeing or talking to him was hard and definitely took its toll. I couldn't believe myself. I'd fucked up and made this thing between us more than it needed to be.

"Who is it?" I asked from the couch.

"It's me Cadence."

"What do you want?"

He said nothing.

"Huh?"

"Can you open the door?"

I sighed standing to my feet to make my way to my door. I took a breath and slowly unlocked the locks, then pulled the door opened taking my time to meet my eyes with his.

"Hey," he said.

"Hi," I said back. Meki had on a pair of basketball shorts and a white tank which meant he planned to turn in for the night.

"Can I come in for a moment?"

I twisted my mouth to one side, thinking.

"Only to talk. I promise." He pressed his right hand to his chest.

I opened the door wide enough for him to step into my apartment.

Usually he would head straight into my bedroom on nights like this but instead he stood with his back pressed to the wall beside the door.

"I'm moving out," he said the moment I closed the door. "Not just out of the building... out of New York."

I furrowed my brows. "All of a sudden? Why?"

"Kurt... he asked me to manage his gym on the west coast. In California," Meki said, referring to celebrity trainer Robert Kurt. He's the owner of the gym I discovered Meki worked out of when I went to redeem my secret Santa gift certificate a year back.

"Business is real good out there. Booming is how everyone is describing it," Meki added.

"I've heard," I mumbled.

"What?"

"Nothing," I replied.

He crinkled his brows then shook his head as if doing that would help him organize his thoughts. "Yeah, so... Kurt opened a private gym a few months back and client sign ups have taken off since then. So he needs someone to manage the whole thing, permanently."

"Wow," I said, trying my hardest to fight my frown. "Well, congratulations."

"I'm prepared to decline the offer," he said closing the space between us, "if you want for me to stay."

"What?"

He released a shaky sigh from his mouth. "I can't believe I'm doing this shit." He dropped his head. "Look, this thing we got going on between us... it turned into something real for me. You may not want to admit that to yourself, but I know you feel it too."

"Meki—"

"Allow me to finish, please."

I gestured for him to continue.

"You told me you loved me and I think you meant what you said."

I shook my head.

"You did, Cadence."

We stared at each other.

"And I didn't want to do that foul shit the other night with Giselle, honestly. But you really pissed me off bringing your ex around here..."

"Meki, you don't have to explain—"

"I'm willing," he interjected while taking my hand, "to stay here and explore a real relationship with you if you ask me not to leave. I'll tell Kurt to find someone else."

I swallowed hard then said, "But this is what you've always wanted... to manage a gym."

"I know—"

"Why would you give that up?"

"There will be other opportunities," he said looking me in my eyes. Meki pressed his hand to my cheek. "But there's only one you, Cae."

I moved my face away from his hand and he sighed.

"Come on Cadence," he said, his voice breaking. "I'm putting my heart out there for you. Meet me halfway, please."

I released a trembling breath.

"Tell me to stay baby, and I will... for you, I will. Without question."

We stood there for a moment, opposite one another. His words stirred in my conscience, tugging at my heart, almost pulling me to say, *yes... stay... don't leave me.*

I wanted to tell him I didn't want him to go. That I loved him but feared being in love again.

Instead of all that I said, "This is an opportunity I believe will only come once."

He briefly dropped his head back between his shoulders. Meki didn't even try to hide he was disappointed.

"You should accept his offer."

"Damn," he said with more breath than tone. Meki stared at me for a moment with a sad look in his eyes. "That fool really fucked you up, huh? Left you jaded as hell for the next man."

He kissed his teeth and reached for my apartment doorknob.

Meki left as quickly as he'd arrived at my place and closed the door behind himself without saying another word.

thirteen

I PACED BACK and forth in my room on a Friday night. Fridays were usually my unofficial holiday, but I'd been dreading this one. It was the night before Meki left Brooklyn.

I thought he was bluffing when he said he had plans to leave. It all became clear he was being real when I saw movers, walking in and out of his apartment each time carrying boxes down the stairs to stack in a waiting UHAUL truck.

That week, I returned to my routine of avoiding Meki.

So, fucking childish, I know.

It was so perplexing trying to understand what kept me from making that move right before he made his move.

My feet padded the floors of my bedroom as I moved about the room. My attempt at organizing my thoughts. Trying to come up with what I'd say after I knocked on his door. I couldn't live with myself if I let him leave without me saying goodbye.

In my head, I debated with if I should tell him I loved him. If I should express those same words when he wasn't inching me closer to a climax. I hoped that was all it was... the reason I screamed I love you in bed. But we hadn't been physical in weeks and I still felt those strong feelings for him.

On my tenth lap in front of my bed, I heard a light knock at my apartment's door. Without even thinking about it, I power walked to my door then paused a foot in front. I reached for the first lock then pulled my hand back, deciding to gather myself before inviting him into the apartment. I took two deep breaths then turned the locks to unlock and open the door.

Meki stood on the other side, his eyes already seeking mine the moment he saw past my door.

We remained at my door for a moment, not saying anything. The look on his face was not that of a man who'd just received a promotion. But not just any promotion, a managerial position in an elite sports club. An establishment that had more fame than its creator, Robert Kurt. This is what Meki had been working so hard to achieve.

He didn't have to work, being an heir to his family's real estate fortune and all. But managing a gym was what he'd been building to gain. Doing so would give him the experience he needed to open his own.

In that moment, I thought back to all those times he shared his dreams and goals with me and I didn't care to listen. How he'd reveal his fears, nonchalantly, and I'd chastise him for wanting to talk when sex was our glue.

My heart ached as we stood apart.

He walked up to me and smoothed his hands from my cheeks to my ears. I closed my eyes and lost myself in his touch. Not wanting to know what my face would be like without him touching me.

He pressed his lips to mine, and I let him. Slipped me his tongue, and I caressed it with mine. After almost a minute of that, he asked on my lips, "Can I come in?"

And I let him.

There was no talking needed. We didn't even bother pretending like we didn't understand the motive behind his visit.

Meki and I wrestled with our clothes, pulling and tugging on each other's shirts and pants until we were close enough to nude.

In bed, we peeled off the rest of our clothing and he peeled open a condom, sheathing his erection.

Inside of me he moved slow, savoring the moment like the seconds were more like hours. For a moment, I put out my mind that this was the last time, his last touch. His last stroke and the last time I'd feel his breath in my ear.

Tears welled in my eyes as Meki tunneled deeper. I spread my legs wider for him, so he'd fill me with more not wanting to miss out on even an inch of him.

"Tell me to stay," he said in my ear but I refused. I couldn't tell this man to give up everything he worked hard for, for a love I wasn't sure I wanted to accept or reciprocate. To gamble on a relationship between him and I working when just a year ago I loathed him.

He pressed his forehead to mine, his mouth agape. I inhaled his exhales and cherished every moment of him being that close. I did it because I knew I'd never be this close to him again.

"Say I'm yours Cadence," he demanded on my lips and I couldn't bring myself to do that either.

"Say it, Cae," he whispered. "Just say it. Please... I need to hear you say it."

Each command I disobeyed his strokes deepened, and I sensed his heart beat weaken.

Never would I have thought a man like him had the potential to reveal this side. So vulnerable. Willing to take a gamble with his heart... with me.

But he was right. I was jaded. This was my heart, my future I'd be risking if I gave in to him.

I wasn't ready to take that chance again.

When we finished, we rested in bed apart, him on his back and me with my back to him. My eyes were wide opened, but I laid still, giving the impression I was asleep.

"Cadence," he said in the dark.

A dim silver glow in the room from the street lamps across the street offered little light. The wind howled outside like a wounded lion, the breeze intrusive, penetrating the gap in my window and sneaking past my thick curtains.

"You up?" he asked next.

I said nothing.

Talking was out of the question. I couldn't trust myself with my words. If he asked me to tell him to stay in that moment I would. I'd say whatever was necessary to keep him in New York. But I wasn't sure about being with him and I didn't want that pressure or guilt. The pressure to prove I was worth passing on a career opportunity and the guilt of knowing he stalled his dream for me. Most importantly, I couldn't take that risk with my heart. Never again.

He moved in closer in bed, pressing his face to the back of my head and inhaling me.

Tears pricked the sides of my eyes as I shut them tight, forcing myself not to cry.

"I love you too, aight?" he whispered. "You probably will never see me say it to your face, but I do."

I did well to steady my breathing as my heart pattered in my chest. Beating harder than any other time as if trying to communicate with me. Doing its best to convince me to reciprocate his words, maybe?

He loved me too. If only that meant something.

"I'll miss you baby," he said next before leaving a kiss on my neck.

Seconds later he stepped off the bed, pulled on his clothes, and left my apartment. He closed my door quietly and the moment it shut, I turned onto my pillow and let the pillowcase have my tears.

Caira was right... I sure fucked this up.

fourteen

JUNE ARRIVED which meant the time for outdoor cocktails and beach bum visits had arrived too. I'd spent so much time indoors during the dry winter months, fantasizing about the heat when it fell below twenty degrees outside. And that warm delightful weather was finally back. We were only in the first week of June but Memorial Day already past, ushering in summer weather.

You would think I'd be eager to step out in a sundress and sandals to let my skin drink the sun's Vitamin D but doing anything adventurous turned me off. During past Junes, it would be impossible to find me between the walls of my apartment. I predicted this season would be different.

Anywhere other than my bed seemed unappealing. Curled up under my blanket with the AC turned up to the max was my version of a comfortable summer morning.

Normally, I would've hit up Caira to see if she wanted to check out brunch or even a matinee. But she kept busy now. She and her baby's daddy were building rapport, realizing the commonalities they shared other than their surprise bundle of joy.

"Y'all are doing everything all backwards," I said to her one night on the phone.

"And happy about it." She laughed. "Chaos is beautiful sometimes."

"Yeah... okay."

Despite my circumstances, seeing her this way made me happy. Caira had never been the relationship type so to see her all doe eyed and speaking French with all her, "we this" and "we that," blew my mind but a good mind-blown. She was changing right before my eyes, blossoming, and the sight forced me to rethink my situation.

Meki left.

I didn't speak with him after our final night together. Not even the next morning before he moved out of Brooklyn for good. Nothing else followed after we spent that night together. And I do mean nothing. No phone calls, texts, social media messages.

The night he tried to convince me to beg him to stay, I wanted to. But I knew my heart wouldn't be in it like his.

Crazy as it sounds, I kind of understood Terrell's hesitation with agreeing to commit to me the way I wanted. Him refusing to be pressured into marriage worked best for him and I respected that because now I found myself in a similar situation.

Meki wanted more than just the occasional hookup. He wanted my heart, my affections, and I refused to give another man that, not again. That took letting my guard down, trusting someone else with my time and my heart and I couldn't bring myself to do it.

I hoped Meki could view things my way and not be disappointed in my decision. He deserved me as a whole person not someone just willing to compromise out of fear of losing him. He wanted love, and I just didn't have it to give. At least I thought I didn't have it to give.

How did something I planned to be only physical turn into this?

Whatever *this* was.

My iPhone ringing made me sit up in bed and reach for it. From an unfamiliar number... the only thing familiar was the area code.

When I answered, it shocked me to hear the voice on the other end.

"Cadence, darling, how are you?" Josephine asked. Even through the phone I could feel her smiling with her words.

"Mrs. Knight? How did you—"

"Get your number? I have my sources." She giggled. "And what did I tell you about that formal Mrs. Knight bit? Josephine will do just fine."

I smiled.

"Listen," she continued. "I want to invite you over for brunch at my home. Same location as the gala. Are you inundated with activities today?"

I chuckled at her properness.

"No, I'm available." I glanced at my closet automatically trying to think of something to wear. "I don't really have an outfit—"

"Darling, come as you are. It'll just be us two."

"Us two?" I echoed.

"I'll let the groundskeepers know to expect you. See you soon, Cadence. Ciao!"

* * *

The Knight's estate was really an amazing palace. Never in my life had I been to a place like this. I'd watched tours of similar mansions on TV but nothing compared to the look in person.

"Hollandaise?" Josephine asked, holding up a small cylinder filled with the homemade yellow sauce for me to take.

I smiled and took it off her hands.

We sat across from each other in a gazebo by their pool. The Olympic-sized pool stretched from one side of the outside property to the other. So behemoth they built its own little house to go with it.

"I didn't get an opportunity to tell you this after the gala," I began, "but your home really is beautiful."

She beamed. "This estate was passed down to my parents by my great grandparents. They owned this along with other properties. Has Meki shared any of our family's history with you?"

I shrugged, pouring some sauce over my eggs. "Not really. Only what I've asked about."

She smiled. "Yes, that sounds like him. He's not very proud of our legacy or our traditions. Many of his friends are nothing like us and he prefers it that way."

Josephine took a sip of her mimosa and looked out in front of herself. "According to tradition, my son should marry a woman who has a family with similar values and wealth."

I nodded.

"Only because that is who we are all around thanks to gatherings like the one I host here. But he branched out to do his own thing, typical of Meki. And in the process, he found you."

I looked away shyly. "Josephine..."

"I got your number from Meki."

My head turned quick in her direction.

"I spoke to him this morning."

"How is he?" I cleared my throat to erase the eagerness wrapped in my words.

"He said he's good. Loves his new place and San Francisco."

"San Francisco," I repeated. The irony. "So that's where he's staying."

She nodded. "But regardless of what he tells me, a mother knows."

I peered over at her.

"He sounded sadder than usual. Like his old self. The Meki I remembered used to sound a lot like the Meki living in California. The weight in his voice lightened a little during the year the two of you dated though."

I sighed.

"He told me about what happened between you two. Explained your relationship."

"It's complicated," I added.

"Darling, that's an understatement."

I snickered.

"I grew up in the 70s. I get it. A time for freedom. But while you're body may be void of emotion, your heart is not."

I blinked my response.

"He told me about what happened at his apartment. His decision to entertain Giselle."

My brows arched. "He told you that?"

She nodded. "He met her at a debutante ball when they were both fifteen. Those types of events were more for business. For the wealthy to flaunt their riches and gain more business, collaborations with like-minded individuals. Giselle's parents attended for traditional reasons, to show the world their daughter in hopes to land her a partner."

I lifted my glass of mimosa to my lips. "Let me guess... Meki was that partner."

"So they wanted. But Meki was not interested. He didn't even want to be there. His father and I... well, more so I, forced him to attend. Giselle had been chasing him for decades."

"Well she got him."

"But he doesn't want her, Cadence."

I sighed and looked away.

"Cadence, the reason I like you is that you're different. Personally, I believe you spend money foolishly on things that are tangible but I'm in no position to judge. You're smart and independent. Brave. Not afraid of how you appear to others."

"That last character trait took time." I giggled. "And that only happened because I gave up on having everything figured out."

The clouds drifted past the sun allowing the rays to shine down in front of us, the gazebo's architectural design shielding us from the harsh light.

"I was in a relationship for a decade and the guy I was with didn't want to take things any further."

Josephine nodded.

"After that relationship, I told myself no more."

"Meki said a similar thing after his relationship."

My brows clumped together. "Relationship? What relationship?"

She chuckled. "You two really shared very little dialog with one another I see."

I dropped my head, a little embarrassed.

"It's all right dear, truly." She smiled. "At nineteen, Meki met a girl at a gala we attended. The daughters of engineers and entrepreneurs were there, most of them seeking his attention, but he refused to be bothered with them. That's because he couldn't take his eyes off one of the servers."

She had my attention after that.

"Her name was Amber. Pretty mulatto girl. Sharp features and high cheek bones. Tall, an aspiring runway model, working as a server to cover bills and photo shoot fees. Her real focus was her modeling career which she struggled to get off the ground."

Josephine stopped to take another sip of her mimosa. "A year into their relationship, Meki realized the girl had troubles she couldn't shake."

"What do you mean?" I asked.

"She had a hard past. Molested by her mother's boyfriend, put out by her mother because of it. Amber secured an apartment at 16-years-old with the lie she was eighteen and waited tables at a local diner by day while modeling at night. She finally caught a break when she landed an agent who booked her on runways and in editorial shoots. But that same agent would betray her. Drugged and raped her one night while the little girl crashed on his couch after an event."

"Oh my God." I brought my hands to my mouth to cup.

Josephine nodded.

"When she and Meki met years later, she'd been through it but there was something in him that made her trust him and she had the same qualities that made him trust her. So they dated for a while, about five years." Josephine sighed. "Five years of suicide attempts, mental breakdowns, and stress they couldn't avoid. When Meki told me his plans to leave the estate to live in an apartment with Amber, I refused to give him my blessing. I liked her, I did, but I knew what she was going through he couldn't fix and that's what he wanted to be, her fixer."

"So what happened?"

"They moved in with one another anyway, for about three months when they were both twenty-four. And things got worse between them. Amber became manic complaining of dreadful night-mares. Their arguments were explosive, sometimes the neighbors would call the authorities to referee."

"Geez."

"Amber had tried to take her life in a variety of ways before and while they dated. The healed slit marks on her wrists were visible during the warmer seasons when it got too hot to keep them hidden."

Josephine sighed and shook her head. "One night she and Meki went to sleep beside one another in bed and he was the only one to wake up in the morning. Amber swallowed a bottle's worth of sleeping pills while he slept and, well..."

"My God." I kept my view down on the gazebo's floor, my eyes shifting. That must have been why it bothered him when I said I'd rather die than to admit I was falling for him.

"I had no idea," I said to Josephine. "He never told me about this."

"Darling, it is not something he likes to discuss, understandably. And as you detailed, your relationship is not one where something like that would have a chance to be discussed."

"Yeah," I said low.

"Since then, Meki has avoided relationships. He acquired female friends by the dozens," she said with finger quotes, "but no one important enough for me to meet, I guess."

We stopped speaking for a moment, using the quiet time to resume eating.

Josephine patted her lips with a napkin then said, "The reason I visited him that day you and I met was because he mentioned you by name the night before."

I looked at her.

"I asked him if he could stop by the mansion to taste a sample of croquettes the caterer considered serving at the gala and Meki declined the visit. He told me, 'I have plans with Cadence.'"

I shrugged a shoulder. "Okay..."

"He never mentions his lady friends by name. Meki always refers to them as, "some girl." When he said your name I had to meet you myself. So I showed up early the next day with some ridiculous excuse about me being in the area. I prayed my reason for the unannounced visit made sense to him so he would let me in and there you walked out into the kitchen with no trousers."

I laughed and so did she.

"Like I said, an interesting first impression."

I smiled.

"Cadence, you two may have had an arrangement that started out as something innocent but I believe it's become something more."

I parted my mouth to speak, but she stopped me with the lift of a finger.

"You don't have to explain. I just want you to think about it yourself. Like I said, Meki... he sounded like his old self again. Bitter, cynical, sarcastic. This past year I've witnessed a metamorphosis in his character and it all clicked for me when he finally mentioned you by name. When he told me how long you've been seeing each other, the shift in his personality made sense. I couldn't put my finger on the change until he confirmed when you two met."

Josephine reached over and took my hand. "Go to him, Cadence. Even just to visit. I'm begging you. I know you've got your work and your life here in New York—"

I giggled nervously while rubbing the back of my neck with my other hand.

"My job offered me a promotion a few months back," I revealed. "To head a department... in San Francisco."

Her brows arched.

"I never told Meki. I wanted to. Even when he told me he was moving there, I wanted to tell him but... I don't know." I released a shaky laugh, my lips quickly falling into a frown.

"Well there you have it, fate," she said slapping her thigh.

"I just don't know if I'm ready, you know? For any of that."

"Well," she said taking another sip of her mimosa. "I can't give you the courage to leap dear. But I can tell you that you only get one life to live so it's important to live it the way you wish. Regrets are time sucks. It's best to make decisions that will bring you closer to happy while minimizing any pains. Meki is in pain right now. He might not admit it but like I said a mother knows. And from the moment I met you, I noticed your pain too."

I sighed.

"My son isn't perfect, but I can assure you he's not your ex-boyfriend either. He's a fool, your ex. My Meki is no fool."

My smile stretched from cheek-to-cheek.

"Consider visiting him in California, Cadence. The drop-in may be just what the two of you need."

I TOOK ALL of Sunday off. Canceled plans with Caira and her beau to check out strollers, refused to plan for the week. Instead, I chose to sit in different parts of my apartment, thinking. Weighing my options and determining what would make me happy while minimizing my pains.

Josephine spoke the truth. I really did have only one life to live and living in fear made life bitter.

The next day, a Monday, I knocked on my supervisor's door just as she arrived in for work.

"Cadence," she said as she took a seat at her desk. "Come in. Please, sit."

"Thank you."

"How was your weekend?" she asked, her focus on her computer as she pushed the power button.

"Insightful."

"Oh?"

I smiled. "I want to take the position in California, if it's still available."

She looked at me with smiling eyes and gave me all of her atten-tion. "Really?"

"Yeah," I said, biting my bottom lip in thought.

Was I really doing this?

My heart beat increased in pace, my palms got clammy. I took a deep breath and ignored all of that. "I want to take a trip out there this week to check the place out. See what housing is available."

I had no idea how I would afford this. My credit cards were damn near over the limit but I'd figure it out.

"That's an excellent plan, Cadence." She pulled out her drawer and handed me a tiny legal notepad. "The company will cover all your expenses. That includes hotel stay, plane tickets, and meals purchased since your trip is work related. Just give us an estimate and keep your receipts during your visit."

My eyes bulged out a little which I corrected quick with a smile. I wouldn't tell her going to Cali wasn't all work related if they offered to foot the bill for my travel and expenses.

"You will love San Francisco," she said smiling big.

"Yeah, I know I will too," I said back.

sixteen

THE NIGHT before I flew out to California I sat at the edge of my bed with my phone in my hand. Josephine told me Meki's number hadn't changed, not yet at least, and I considered calling him. I wanted to let him know I would be in his town but every time I clicked into my contacts and readied myself to click his name to call; I stopped.

No amount of deep breaths could remedy it. I still feared taking that step with him.

But why?

I knew it was silly. And really I was letting Terrell win by allowing our breakup to dictate my make up with Meki.

The other part of me worried if Meki would have me after everything that went down between us. The man poured his heart out. Stepped out of himself to show me he wanted more and each time I swatted him away. No one would take that type of rejection over and over and not lose interest after a while.

I stood to my feet and walked back and forth in front of my bed. To my left were my luggage, two suitcases. I planned to spend a week in Cali. I figured that was enough time to find a decent place and to learn the area well enough so my first seven days living there wasn't a disaster.

This was different, this thing I was getting ready to do. Move to a different part of the country. I lived nowhere else besides the east coast. This part of the U.S. has always been home. Now I was going 3,000 miles away. Stepping into the unknown with no idea how any of this would pan out. But I needed this change and truthfully I needed Meki.

Instead of calling him, I tapped into my safari app and typed in Robert Kurt's name with the term San Francisco.

The first few results consisted of news articles written by reporters who attended the official re-opening of the gym. The second my eyes fell on Meki's photo in the write-up, my heart melted.

My mind wandered to our final night together. How he felt, the words he expressed so freely. He told me he loved me and that thought made a smile pull at my lips.

Write-ups from online magazines were favorable, a lot of them consisting of the names of celebrities and big named people who exercised at the gym.

The funds in my checking account were low. The only credit card not over the limit had only four hundred dollars available. I used all of that to buy a day pass for the facility, deciding to surprise Meki instead of letting him know I would be in San Francisco.

I hoped my decision was a wise one.

* * *

The weather in California proved to be different. Pleasant, breezier, but still sunny. San Francisco was no Brooklyn, and I appreciated the contrast in locations.

The first thing I noticed after leaving the airport and hopping in the cab were the steep rolling hills. The streets seemed to be full of hills and slopes. Cars drove up or down those hills. Homes looked like they were leaning against one another and the fog in the air was thicker than nicotine clouds.

I booked a hotel downtown, so my driver had to drive through some surrounding areas to get there. We passed through the city's version of China Town. I pressed my face to the window like an excited kid and peered up above us. Overhead were tiny golden yellow flags along with red lanterns swinging by sturdy strings and dangling in the wind.

The sounds of cable cars and trolleys rolling and dinging over man-made street tracks was as common as pigeon calls in New York.

The air in San Francisco smelled fresher, cleaner and already I felt my mood elevate the longer we drove.

My driver dropped me off in front of the Hilton located downtown. Here the buildings were just as tall as the ones in New York. They differed in their shapes. San Francisco architects designed the buildings in the shape of triangles, much like the Flatiron building in NYC. The buildings in San Francisco all formed at a point, an angle.

Up in my hotel room, after checking out the room and inspecting the bed sheets, I reached for my suitcase prepared to take out all of my clothes to put away. I stopped myself. New city, new ways. I went out and enjoyed the scenery instead. And my first stop would be visiting Meki at the gym to let him know I'd arrived in his new town.

* * *

The moment I stepped off the elevator and onto the main floor of Robert Kurt's San Francisco gym, I smiled. The place looked amazing... just as amazing as Robert's gym in New York. I'd worked out at his gym in Manhattan, even had the pleasure of finally meeting Robert with the help of Meki.

I approached the desk, gave the receptionist my name, and she confirmed my entrance.

"Is Meki Knight working today?" I asked.

She nodded. "Yes, but he's booked all month."

I smiled, pleased. Of course he was booked. He was one of the best.

"Did you want to sign up for a session for next month?"

"No that's fine, thank you."

She smiled back. "You're all set. The ladies' locker room is behind you and to the right. Enjoy your workout!"

With my things locked away in a locker, I stepped out of the changing room with my intensions set on running into him before he saw me. He was always great at sneaking up on me, having one over on me. I wanted to be the wiser this time.

As I searched the faces, anticipation for seeing him after being apart for the past few weeks built within. I wondered what our first words to each other would be. How receptive he would be to see me there. I was more excited than nervous though.

I finally spotted him as we stood feet away from each other. He'd just finished up with a client, a guy who resembled an athlete based on his build and height.

"I'll see you next week," Meki said to his client as the guy gave him a pound and walked away.

I watched as Meki sat the gallon of water he'd been carrying on the floor beside his right foot as he stood over a makeshift desk, filling out paperwork attached to a clipboard.

I made my way over, fighting back my smile while taking a deep breath.

Close, I approached the wall ahead of him and pressed my back against the cool surface. He kept his focus down on the form he wrote on until I said, "It's hard to get a session with you, huh?"

He glanced up at me and did a double take.

I shrugged. "I mean, it's not like I could afford you or whatever."

"I..." He cleared his throat. "I'd train you for free. You know that."

We stared at each other for a moment, me fighting back my tears and him finding it impossible to hold back his smile.

"Hi," I said then released a shaky exhale. "I thought about calling you to let you know I'd be in town but maxing out my credit card to get a day pass made better sense."

He laughed, bringing his palm to his lips and running it down slow.

"Wow," he said, his eyes stuck on mine. "I can't believe you're here right now. What are you doing here?"

I giggled. "I'm here for work so I figured I'd stop by and say hi. So... hi." I moved in closer and he licked his lips. "So far, San Francisco looks good. Like home."

"Meki," the receptionist called from the desk. "Your next client just arrived."

"Yeah," he said back. "Thanks."

"So busy." I grinned.

"I'll reschedule with them."

"No." I shook my head. "It's difficult to book you. Rescheduling will crush the person who's already here for their session."

He sighed. "Okay... well it'll be two hours until I'm free. How long are you in town? Where are you staying?"

"The Hilton."

He shook his head. "That place is trash. Wait here for a moment, I'll be right back."

Meki turned and jogged toward a room, disappearing behind the door. I walked closer and saw it was an office, a really nice office with an incredible view of the bay. I beamed, impressed.

"Here," he said walking back over with his hand extended and holding a set of keys. "Go to my place." I took the keys, and he walked to that makeshift desk again and ripped off a piece of blank paper.

"This is my address," he said, as he wrote. Meki handed me the paper then pulled out his phone, unlocked it then tapped on an app. "I'm calling you a black car to take you over there. Go straight there, aight?"

I smiled.

"Promise me you'll go straight there," he said, pressing his hand to my cheek.

I nodded then said, "After I get my bags, yes. I promise."

He ran the pad of his thumb over the thickest part of my lower lip then folded his lips into his mouth. "I'd destroy you right now if I didn't have to be professional and shit."

I burst out laughing.

"Damn," he said, stepping back. "I can't believe you're here."

"Meki," the receptionist called from the desk. "They're waiting."

"Be right there," he said back, his eyes still on me. "I'll see you in a few hours, aight?"

I nodded.

He walked away, backwards, his eyes still on me. "You promised," he said. "Keep your word."

"I will."

"And Cadence?"

"Yes."

He licked his lips slow. "Please... don't have anything on when I get home."

I slacked my jaw, my lips pulling up in a smile as I watched him turn and walk away. I held his keys in my hand and made my way toward the locker room, eager to see how the day would end.

seventeen

THE BLACK CAR ride to Meki's home was a quick one. He didn't live very far from the gym, so the destination literally was walking distance if you compared it to getting around New York.

The neighborhood was gorgeous once I got past the front gate. The homes were built real modern and sophisticated. This wasn't your average white picket fence properties or even *Full House* townhouses. They resembled homes seen on episodes of Miami Vice. Architecturally modern and sleek. This was definitely his style.

When I got in front of his home, my jaw dropped. Standing outside I could already tell the house was about two-stories tall with a lot of space. Obviously not the Knight's estate but a nice compromise for Ms. Nice.

I giggled at the thought.

His home like all the other homes in the area sat on a hill. It had protruding clerestory windows. You know the type, with wide, clear panes high above eye level. Gorgeous.

I stepped in front of his door and inserted the key, unlocking the lock. With the door opened, I automatically inhaled the scent of his cologne lingering in the air. The space had a cool 21st century look to it with narrow walkways, high-ceilings and a bunch of green living design elements. Meki kept the lights off in the home but the space was lit up. Natural light cast such a beautiful glow over the entry way, inviting me in further.

Straight ahead of me was his staircase that I assumed led up to the bedrooms. So that's where I went first. As soon as I got to the top of the stairs, I noticed the three doors leading to the bedrooms. I walked past them and noticed they all had outdoor terraces, offering views of the city and water.

Those windows I mentioned looked even better from inside the house. They resembled picture frames capturing the beauty of San Francisco.

"Wow, this is so dope," I said to myself. "What else does this place have?"

I stepped down the stairs, breathing in the filtered fresh air.

I made my way through the kitchen, admiring the sleek white marble counters doubling as an eating area. Steel stools with cushioned backings sat pushed under the opposite island. The doors behind it opened out to an outside area decorated with a chair and table. An outdoor hot tub sat a few feet away.

"What!" I said out loud. I walked over to it and sat beside the tub. It was bigger than your usual hot tub. Clearly this didn't come with the property. Meki must have had this one installed on his own.

"Beautiful," I said as I stood out there, inhaling the air and smiling so hard I could barely hold my lips up.

I pulled out my phone and dialed up Caira. I told her my plans to travel to California for work but she had no idea I was coming here to see Meki too. She would flip.

"Hello?" she said on the other end.

"Hey, cuzzo." I glided my hand along the outdoor table, pulling out a chair to take a seat. "Guess where I'm at?"

"Cali. You told me you were going a few days ago."

"Yes, I'm in Cali but I'm somewhere in particular."

"Where?"

I beamed. "Meki's."

She screamed. "Wait, Meki, Meki?"

"The only Meki we know."

"What you doing over there?"

I smiled. "Trying to fix things."

"That's my girl."

We laughed.

"So, what are you thinking of doing to fix things? How you about to get your man back?"

Her referring to him as that, my man, made me blink back tears.

"He told me not to have anything on when he gets home. So..."

"Ooohhhh," she gushed. "I like that."

"But," I said, peeking over my shoulder at the hot tub, "I got something else he might like better."

eighteen

I HEARD him the moment he walked through the door and felt myself get all giddy. He had two sessions that afternoon, each one an hour long, so he arrived at his place soon after finishing with them.

The sun was prepared to set in half-an-hour and I wanted to check out the scenery more before night fell.

"Cadence?" he shouted. The sound of him dropping his gym bag to the floor by the door sent an echoing thud around the space.

"Yeah," I replied. I made my way out of his room where I'd been hanging out since my arrival and over to the top of his stairs.

He threw his hands up in the air when he saw me fully dressed. "I thought I told you—"

"I know." I blushed. "But you owe me a workout."

Meki chuckled. He walked to the foot of the stairs and started his ascend to me and I looked away shyly.

"I can give you a workout up here, right now if you like."

I giggled.

"Come here," he said in front of me. "I've been waiting two very long hours to do this." He cradled my jaw in his hands then pressed his lips to mine. His kiss reminded me of breathing in air after holding my breath for so long. My legs almost weakened by his touch. He just felt right. Yet and still I pulled away and stepped back a step.

"What?"

"Let's go running."

"Running? For what?"

"I stopped by the gym for a workout. Hoped you had room to take me."

"Here," he said taking my hand and walking up the stairs ahead of me. "Let me stretch you out upstairs."

I refused to move. "Meki."

He grunted.

"Please."

He closed his eyes and released a deep sigh. "Fine. You want to do a quick run around the neighborhood?"

"No." I grinned. "Do you know of any parks?"

The San Francisco Bay Park looked more like a place people went to hike. Large rolling hills, more dirt than pavement. The place was an outdoorsy person's dream.

Our Nike sneakers kicked up the dirt as we ran along the trail. Whipping by trees the wind breezing past our faces. I did my usual breathe in through my nose and out through my mouth. Everything to keep up with Meki.

He looked over at me and smiled and I couldn't help but to return one back.

"How long are you in town for?" he asked through his breaths.

"Until Monday," I exhaled. "But I'll be back."

We turned the curve and headed down a hill, slowing our pace.

"I'm here for work," I added. "They offered me a promotion a few months ago."

He stopped running for a moment something I only realized a few feet ahead of him. I turned to face him.

"Come on," I said, stopping and jogging in place to maintain my heart rate. "Let's keep running."

"What kind of promotion?" he asked, still frozen in place.

"Resource Director here in San Francisco."

Meki walked up to me, sweat beads rolling down his arms, his chest heaving as I'm sure his heart rate tried to steady itself. "You're moving out here?"

I stopped jogging and nodded.

Sweat pooled in my cleavage and slicked my face, exactly what I hoped would happen.

He smiled big then used my hand to pull me close. "They offered you a promotion months ago, and you didn't tell me that?"

I shrugged. "I was still deciding. But then you moved out to Cali, San Francisco of all places, and I just—"

He pressed his lips to mine, our breaths heavy from both running and desire.

Meki pulled away briefly then bent his legs at the knees, picking me up and tossing me over his shoulder.

"Let's forget all this running," he said carrying me in the opposite direction of where we were running. "We're going home."

"Meki," I said through my laughs. "Let's finish."

"Nah," he said moving closer toward his car. "We'll finish the right way at home."

* * *

It took a little convincing, but I got Meki to agree to shower together.

"You don't need a shower," he said, following me up his stairs once we were inside the house. "I'm sure you're already wet."

"But I'm all sweaty," I said, glancing at him over my shoulder.

"I'll take you as you are."

I smiled, peeling off my shirt and dropping it to the floor.

"Mmm," he said, doing the same.

We left trails of our clothing from the stairs to the bathroom where we stood under the sprinkling shower head, cleansing our skins, our eyes roaming our figures. Meki and I looked at each other like we were seeing one another for the first time.

He lathered my arms and legs with soap and I soaped his back. His hands on me a honeyed reminder of the times we shared in New York.

For once, I had no walls up. Finally there in the moment and lost in his touch.

The longer I made us wait for it the more in need we both became. Meki stood in front of me, water trailing down his tawny-brown skin and splashing against his hard-on.

I closed the space between us, gripped him there while bringing my lips to his.

We kissed, smacking noises echoing around his stand-in shower. Our moans substituted where the sloshing noise of the water spilling from the shower head missed.

I lowered myself down in front of him and invited the length of him into my mouth whole. Hallowed my cheeks around his erection as I bobbed back and forth below him.

He watched me the entire time, running his wet hands through my hair and dropping his head back when the pleasure I served him got real good. I found my rhythm and swirled my tongue as I bobbed. I thought I would come from only pleasing him. My hair would be a frizzy mess by sunrise but I didn't care. I wasn't about to sweat the small stuff anymore. It was all about him.

He spilled his cream over my lips. I let it drip to my breasts as I continued to tickle the head of his staff with the tip of my tongue.

Meki pressed his hands to the shower wall high above my head and roared his pleasure around the bathroom.

It was the sweetest sound.

After a quick rinse, I propositioned him to step outside to his hot tub.

Night had fallen as I'd planned. Surely at that hour, his neighbors had already returned home from work. But again, I didn't care. I was void of worry about who might hear us or even see us in the act.

Wrapped in separate towels, we filled the tub up and when there was enough water, I dropped my towel and stepped in first. He followed. Once submerged in water, he pressed his lips to my neck and licked me from the lobe of my right ear to my collarbone, never stopping his decent.

He tongued my nipples, one at a time, sucking on them briefly before his hands gripped each side of my waist tight.

Meki lifted me high enough for me to sit at the hot tub's edge and slid me close to him. I was at his mouth's level when he pushed through the water, canceling even more space between us to place a kiss on my lower lips.

"Let me return the favor," he said, spreading my thighs farther apart so he could flick his tongue along the tip of my clit.

He licked and sucked me to a shaking climax and didn't stop when I told him I was coming. Kept on whipping his tongue back and forth, burying his lips between my folds and playing a disappearing act with his tongue inside of me as I coated that tongue with my tang.

I hiked my right leg up, balanced it on the tub's edge, and rode his face as he met my pelvic thrusts with his mouth. He helped me to grind harder by holding me by the waist. Moving in even closer and rotating my pink nub with the swirl of his tongue, only stopping when I shuddered on his lips again.

He guided me down into the tub, the warm water feeling just right against my heat. His lips were on mine as he delved into me, gripping his shaft with his hand and guiding himself in long enough for my walls to welcome him further.

The water was our mattress as it helped with his strokes. Splashing around us in that tub moving in time with his pumps. Meki looked me right in my eyes as he made me submit. Each time I found it hard to watch him, to keep focused as he pleased me. He told me, "Don't look away. Keep them on me."

But that was only for a little

He finished me off by turning me around to serve me from the back. His hands in my hair again using it to pull me on and off his dick. My moans were far from silent and he didn't bother to muffle them. In fact, when I leaned forward against the edge of the tub to press my lips to my forearm to mask my cries, he pulled me farther away from the edge

"No. Don't hold back," he growled, continuing to drill in and out of me even faster from the back. "Let the neighbors know baby..."

The sound of our wet bodies meeting echoed around us, accompanying our moans and groans.

"Let them know how good I'm being to you tonight, Cae."

And when I came, I came hard. Felt everything. The contractions around his dick, the explosion teetering on the edge. The sensation of pushing my climax on him as it swept through me and made me weak. All of my boundaries uncoiled with it. The walls I'd built tumbled and reduced to ashes of nothingness. He had me opened, and I loved it.

Meki wrapped his arm around me and pressed his free hand to the tub's edge to hold me up in the water.

He grunted, his body shuddered some more with each last pump he delivered.

We both shook with me in his arms, gasping for air that was in abundance out there. But we were drowning on one another. Blissfully. Fully willing to stay there together. I tensed up and so did he and when we reached that point of no return, we arrived at the same time. It was like music. A duet. The world could end and it wouldn't matter with us that connected. Nothing beat that synchronicity in that moment.

It felt like being hollowed out then recharged with shocks and currents. That spark blasting us on a wave of ecstasy. And when we came back down to earth, he leaned his chest against my back then pulled me down into the water, onto him. As I continued to pulse around his erection, Meki wrapped his arms so tight around me I believed he'd never let me go. He pressed his lips to my back and panted while planting kisses there.

I caught my breath and got the courage I needed to part my lips and say, "I love you Meki."

He moved from behind to in front of me to look me in the eyes.

"I love you," I repeated, smiling. "I'm in love with you. I took a while to admit that but... yes, I do and yes I am in love. And I want you to know that..."

He pressed his finger to my lips to stop me from continuing. "I love you too Cadence. For a long time now I've been in love with you."

My smile grew wider when he moved in for a kiss.

I remembered in that moment being in bed with him his final night in New York. Me faking sleep and him expressing his love for me. He also said he'd probably never be able to say it to my face.

I'm happy that was a lie.

The irony of things, huh? I guess the saying is true... never say never. Because when you make plans, God laughs.

Surely when it came to the plans I had for Meki when I believed we were only hooking up, God must have laughed hard enough to get hiccups.

epilogue

"WELCOME, family, friends and all loved ones," the pastor said in front of Meki and me.

Swaying palm trees surrounded us. The breeze swept over our skins, the sun highlighted our melanin complexions, and sand powdered our toes.

Meki and I glanced at each other and smiled, my heart full with so much love and delight.

"We gather here today to witness the union of these two amazing souls," the pastor continued.

Meki took my hand in his and winked.

"And to celebrate the wedding of..."

I folded my lips into my mouth and blushed.

"Caira and Dwayne."

No, it's not my wedding. Not yet, at least.

My man and I sat under the setting sun in Cancun, Mexico. Meki and I grabbed seats near the front of the aisle, watching as my cousin Caira took vows with her soon to be husband, Dwayne.

Married. Wow. I never thought Caira would jump the broom before me but I wasn't mad at it either.

"You have come here to sunny Mexico to share in this commitment Caira and Dwayne have chosen to make to one another..."

For October, the weather was gorgeous out here, but I was happy with the climate in San Francisco too.

Yeah, I was officially a Californian. Never did I think I had it in me to pack everything up and just leave New York not only for work, but for love too.

"You are here," the pastor added, "to offer your love and support to this union, and to allow Caira and Dwayne to begin their married journey together surrounded by the people nearest and dearest to them. But most important, those who have a special place in their hearts."

My cousin was officially seven months pregnant with a baby girl but you couldn't tell. She'd always been thin, and it was about to work to her benefit. Her wedding photos would be poppin'.

I watched her stand ahead of us, blushing and glowing, dressed in a flowing white off the shoulder gown with a tail that blew in the wind. She looked like an Egyptian queen, with the pink and white flower crown to match.

Only fifteen people were invited including Caira's parents and mine. My mother refused to miss this wedding even if she hated flying in planes.

"So welcome to one and all," the pastor continued, "who have traveled from near and far places. Caira and Dwayne thank you."

Caira looked over at me and winked. She stuck out her tongue and made a silly face next. I laughed at the sight.

"That's gonna be us soon," Meki said in my ear before leaving a kiss there.

He sent a chill down my spine that made me shiver.

Meki.

Things had gotten even better between us after that night in his house. The man was ready to put a ring on it as we sat across from each other at breakfast the day after my arrival to California.

"Marry me," he told me. "I'll get a diamond by noon."

I laughed, forking eggs into my mouth. "Is that what you want?"

He smiled at me, "absofuckinglutly."

Meki was so ready, he suggested we go to the courthouse to make it official. I wanted marriage, but not that quick. My parents would kill me if they weren't allowed to bear witness to our union. Besides, Meki and I needed to get to know each other better, romantically and on purpose. We'd already seen the bad in one another. Now it was time for the good.

So instead, we settled on an engagement without the ring. That stuff just didn't matter anymore. I realized somehow a true union meant more than material things. It was what happened, how we dealt with situations after we said "I do" that mattered most.

I found a place out in Cali and made it home number two. Meki insisted I live with him but I still liked my space. Plus, having two places to shack up at added that much desired fire to our union. Having him in my life made it easy for me to appreciate my days more. I'm thankful.

"They thank you for your presence here today," the pastor finished. "And now they ask for your blessing, encouragement, and lifelong support, for their decision to be married."

Meki and I planned to have a chilled wedding much like this one which the old me would've protested against. Against having a simple ceremony and reception, against being engaged without a ring my fiancé had no problem affording... he is an heir. Hell, I'd even be against falling in love again. But here we were, together, in love, and ready for the next chapter of our lives.

We were at my cousin's wedding. A cousin who hated the title "Wifey" once upon a time.

Change was real.

Change was good.

And I liked the change I finally allowed into my life.

Meki leaned over and kissed me on the neck making me giggle like a school girl.

"You're looking too damn good sitting here next to me."

I glanced down at his pale gray stretch linen suit, biting my bottom lip. "You look even better."

"When we get back to the room," he said, moving close to my ear to whisper, "I want all of this right here... off and on the hotel room's floor."

"Ditto."

Life is interesting that way isn't it?

Working itself out and giving you what you want just not in the way you would have expected. And I was fine with that. Okay with things not going as planned. Going with the flow even when the change in plans seemed random. On most days my smile couldn't be contained. I was finally happy. Thrilled for the future even.

For once, everything was nice... A Cadence kind of nice, except totally unexpected. Turns out, not getting what I thought I wanted with my ex Terrell, ended up being a fabulous stroke of luck.

The End.

<h1 style="text-align:center">final words</h1>

Hey Reader!

Thank you so much for reading *A Love Deferred*! Cadence and Meki's love story has been a story I've had brewing in my mind for some time now. It all started after typing "The End" at the conclusion of their short story *Unsilent Knight*.

When I first worked on that story, I wanted to offer something for the Christmas holiday that wasn't too holiday-esque. After publishing *Unsilent Knight*, most readers wanted a full novel for these two. Though their story was a beautiful one, I wasn't confident I could carry out their love journey throughout a novel. So I compromised and developed this novella. Truthfully, their story wasn't really over at the end of *Unsilent Knight*. They kept talking. But I had a long list of other stories to tell, stories I published in 2018 and stories that are coming in 2019 and onward, but I digress lol.

Their story in *Unsilent Knight* wasn't a "happily ever after" many are used to. It was their version of a happily ever after... for now, one that had some readers wanting more which I hope *A Love Deferred* satisfied.

For this novella, I wanted to pick up where we left off at in the short story and show just what happens when two strong characters, both alpha, attract one another. I debated with myself on calling this an enemies-to-lovers novella. I didn't feel it would be a justified label since in *Unsilent Knight* it was clear but in *A Love Deferred* it became one-sided.

Cadence as a character was to go against all the qualities of a main character in a romance who instead of running toward love was doing everything to avoid it. But even she couldn't run far enough. I also wanted to turn the tables on the typical "situation-ship." Women are usually the ones pushing for a man to take them seriously, settle down, and make things official. Today, the roles are different. Women are more independent and content not having a label and I looked to capture this in Cadence and Meki's story.

I also wanted to show that a man can be an alpha, a bit arrogant and "macho" but still be in touch with his feelings and open with his heart. To not fear putting his heart out there even knowing there's a chance it could get stomped on. You don't see that a lot and that appealed to me, inspiring me to pen this story.

Being in love is an attractive vulnerability to some and takes a lot of strength. Strength of the heart and the mind. Understanding the risk you take giving your heart to someone and hoping they know what to do with it, takes a lot of trust and courage, something Meki was more than ready for but that Cadence was fearful of giving into. Showing Meki's vulnerable side with Cadence was something I really wanted to include in the story. You see him always asking her if she wants him and for her to tell him that she belonged to him. These were all cries for validation, for her to validate him and their growing bond.

My goal with this story was to show a unique way of falling in love. Not everyone falls in love the same way and happiness isn't determined by doing everything in a way deemed "right." We have enough examples of what happens when people do things "right" and how things still don't work in their favor.

Cadence and Meki's love was unexpected. And Cadence believed her breakup with her boyfriend was a terrible thing since she had goals of marriage and a family. But eventually even she realized something viewed as a negative or a delay in one's goals can often be perfect in God's plans. As the saying goes, "If God is making you wait, expect more than what you asked for."

Thank you again for reading. If this is your first time reading a story by me, welcome! You are now what I like to call a Brookelynite. To my current reading family, I appreciate your continued support. You inspire me to always offer and be my best.

See you at the end of the next book!

Love,

Brookelyn.

about the author

Brookelyn Mosley is a captivating voice in the world of black romance literature. With a gift for weaving heartfelt narratives and steamy encounters, she invites readers on journeys of love, passion, and self-discovery. Through her compelling storytelling, Brookelyn celebrates the beauty of black love and explores the complexities of relationships with authenticity and depth. With over 50+ titles, her stories resonate with true-blue readers, touching hearts and inspiring conversations about love, identity, and resilience.

Connect With Me Online!

Facebook: http://facebook.com/brookelynmosley
Facebook Reading Group: Brookelynites Book Lounge
Instagram: @Brookelynmosley
My Website: BrookelynMosley.com
My Readers Website: BKBookLounge.com
My Mailing List: BK Insiders

9 781965 507438